ROAR

CATNIP ASSASSINS BOOK 7

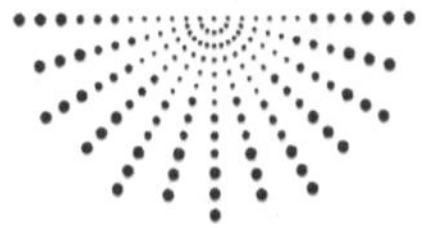

SKYE MACKINNON

Peryton Press

It's time for the last meow.

Her whole life, Kat has been fighting for survival. For her freedom.

Now she's done. She wants peace. Even if that means having to risk everything she loves.

The final book in this purrfectly exciting urban fantasy series full of action, suspense and cat puns. A slow burn reverse harem where Kat won't have to choose.

A QUICK WORD BEFORE WE GET STARTED

As you will know from the previous books, this series is set in a world very similar to our own, but there are some deciding differences. Technology has developed differently, and while there are many devices you may be used to, such as televisions, there are no mobile phones, cars or the internet. No guns, either.

This book is written in British English and uses some British expressions and idioms. Please don't see these as spelling mistakes. We say mum rather than mom, use a lot of 's' instead of 'z' (cosy, realise, ...) and use 'got' as the past participle of 'get' (instead of 'gotten').

And finally, subscribe to Skye's newsletter for updates about new releases: skyemackinnon.com/newsletter.

You'll even get a free book for subscribing, so it's totally worth it.

For Sootie, my little demon/cat.
You've helped Kat reach the final meow.

Kat has been catnapped (although she calls it self-kidnapped) and is being tortured, starved and left in isolation. After months of abuse, she finds herself in a new room instead of her cell. Of course, she tries to escape, but she gets stopped by mutant goons every time. She meets a mouse called Whiskers and is surprised she's able to communicate with the rodent. Together, they hatch out an escape plan, but before they can put it into practice, Kat's clone sister visits her. She calls herself Sophie and while she's clearly been brainwashed, she's also an intelligent and sometimes kind girl.

With a bit of manipulation from Kat, the two of them escape and get in touch with Lily, who directs them to a village where they might get to meet Kat's mates. Before they manage to get there, however, they are ambushed by servants of Lord Delaney, Sophie's adoptive father. Kat shifts and goes feral for quite a bit, until Ryker and Lennox find her. In the process of getting her to shift back, they all end up naked and have some reunion fun.

When they're all finally reunited, everything seems purrfect – until Kat realises she's pregnant with four babies. Her pregnancy proceeds rapidly and they never make it back to Attenburgh.

Claw ends with our heroes surrounded by Lord Delaney and his men, Kat's waters broken and well, everything looks very bad…

PROLOGUE

LADY LARA

I stare at the coin on my desk. Bronze, with a square in the centre that's cut through in the middle with a sharp vertical dash. It's not the first Fang coin reaching me and it won't be the last. They're more active again. As soon as I discover one and put them to justice, yet more appear.

The Fangs are everywhere. Kat told me once how they'd been involved in killing shifter children in her hometown. It's only one of many examples of their twisted, cruel ideology. Most of them are sirens - and everyone in charge most definitely is one of those creatures - but they also have some humans in their employ. I don't know why a human would want to work for an organisation that wants to rule over us, but the temptation of power can make people do horrible things.

I pick up the coin and turn it in my hands. It's heavier than it looks. It was found on the body of a young woman. I've been shown a picture of her bloodied corpse. She looked human, but that doesn't mean anything. Unless shifters are killed in their animal form, their bodies look just as human as you and me. Kat's Ryker is the only exception. His golden eyes give him away as a non-human, but after hearing how he grew up as a cat and didn't even know he was a shifter, I can understand that he's a little different.

The dead woman is special not just because of the coin, but because she was found in an alley behind the town hall. Unlike other parts of Attenburgh, this is a safe area, well-guarded and policed. Murders don't happen here. Until now. This is the second death in the vicinity of my office this week.

It's a message, I'm sure of it. The Fangs are challenging me. The previous mayor was happy to turn a blind eye and I have my suspicions that he accepted bribes, but I'm not him. I follow the rules, even if that means going against some of the most powerful people in the country.

With a sigh, I dial the M.E.O.W. headquarters' number. It's rare that one of them is home, not with Kat missing, but I may be lucky for once. I could sure use some luck just now.

"Yes?" a tired male voice asks. Benjamin, if I'm correct. I've got to know all the M.E.O.W. members rather well during Kat's absence. I've been trying to help find her, but until a few days ago, she'd seemed to have vanished off the face of the Earth. Now she's finally been found, but I don't know when she'll get back to Attenburgh.

"It's the mayor. Is Lily around?"

"Nope, I'm the only one. How can I help?"

He yawns, not even trying to hide his exhaustion. I think they're all at the brink of collapse. Kat disappeared months ago, and they've not only been trying to find her ever since, but have also worked hard to keep the business afloat. I've given them as many paid contracts as I could, but I need to be careful not to look like I have favourites. In theory, I should put out everything to tender, but I don't usually bother for the small stuff. Or anything to do with my personal security. I should probably up my protection after the woman was found dead.

"Are you aware of any increased Fang activity?" I ask Benjamin.

He gulps audibly. "No. Why?"

"There's been two murders. Definitely the work of the Fangs, they left their bronze coins. Let me know if you hear anything. I don't want them getting a hold again in my town."

"Of course, Lady Lara. Do you think they're connected to the siren who kidnapped Kat?"

"I'm starting to believe that everything is connected in one way or another. Any news of Kat?"

"No, they must still be on the way here. It shouldn't be much longer though. Last I heard they were in some backwater village waiting for the weather to get better. I'll get in touch as soon as she's back."

I flip the coin to distract myself from my worry. "Do that. And keep an eye out for anything that could be the Fangs' doing."

I end the call and lean back, tightening my fingers around the heavy coin. I feel like something is about to happen; an eery premonition that causes shivers to run down my back. With the exception of Kat's disappearance, the past few months have been quiet. Maybe too quiet. I hope this isn't the calm before the storm, but something tells me that this hope is in vain.

I need to be vigilant and ready for whatever is to come.

CHAPTER ONE

Blood runs down my legs. Blood pools on the ground. And blood is splattered all over my face.

I don't care. The only thing that matters is the pain. I'm being torn apart from the inside. I'm on all fours, panting, trying to stay conscious. Around me, the battle rages. I wish I could help, but I'm incapacitated. I just have to hope the guys can prevail despite us being outnumbered.

I cry out when another wave of red-hot pain tears through my abdomen. I wouldn't be surprised if my babies are trying to claw their way outside, ignoring the usual birthing process. Was this Delaney's plan? Me dying in childbirth? I bet he wouldn't mourn me even if it hadn't been his intention.

My cat is close to the surface, urging me to shift. But I can't. I don't know what that would mean for the kittens inside of me. They could get hurt, and even though they're giving me more pain than I've ever felt before, I don't want them harmed. I'll put them in the naughty corner once they're born. That's the deal.

Gryphon shouts something in the distance. I look up, but he's hidden behind the wall of twitching limbs and splattering blood. Around me is chaos, no, carnage. It's a fight to the death and all participants are willing to kill their enemies. I can't spot Delaney either. I imagine he's somewhere removed from the battle, watching, letting his mutants do the dirty work for him. He doesn't look like a fighter. He's a politician, a manipulating slimy siren.

The next wave of agony makes me collapse to the ground. I want to curl up, but my giant belly is in the way. Why do women do this voluntarily? This will be the first and last time I ever give birth. I'll neuter my males as soon as this is over.

Back at the Pack, I once watched a woman give birth. She was one of the shifters who had more freedom than us collared children. They'd organised a midwife for her and I was tasked to help with whatever was needed. I still don't know why; there were much more compliant kids than me. The midwife's voice rang in my head. *Breathe through the pain. You're stronger than you think.*

I'd stab her memory if I could. She's likely never had four clawed beings in her uterus. I imagine them ripping apart my insides and shudder. But I don't have time to linger on the image. Pain crashes over me. The contractions are getting faster. I must be close. The sooner this is over, the better.

"Kat!" Sophie shouts from somewhere behind me. "Watch out!"

I turn, far slower than I usually would, just in time to see a giant launch himself at me. He's wielding an axe that's longer than me. I roll to my side, try to jump to my feet, but my balance is off and my massive bump makes me far heavier than I'm used to. I trip and land back on all four, but luckily, that means I just about evade the swipe of his axe. I throw myself forward, grab his ankles and pull with all my strength. He doesn't even sway. Fuck.

My uterus chooses that moment to give me another contraction and I howl in pain. The mutant doesn't care. He hauls out again, sending the axe whirling at me-

Something small hits him from the side and he stumbles, out of balance. The axe's blade slices into my shoulder, but it's only a graze. I'll take that over a beheading any day.

He growls as a small knife glints in the sunlight before it embeds itself in his neck. Correction: Sophie embeds it in his neck. She's clinging to him like a monkey and he stares at her in surprise before falling backwards. She jumps off him just before he hits the ground and lazily retrieves her knife. It's one the cook gave us. If I ever see that woman again, I'll hug her. And give her a large bag of money.

I want to thank Sophie, but another contraction tears through me and blurs my vision. I can't do this for much longer. When the pain fades a little, I look down at my legs. My thighs are covered in blood. Something's wrong.

"We're winning!" Sophie calls out. "What shall I do?"

"Where's Delaney?" I grunt just when the next wave of pain hits me. I squeeze my eyes shut and the memory of that midwife appears. *When you feel the need to push, push. And pant.*

No, I don't feel the need to push. I feel the need to kill everyone around me just to make me forget this pain.

"Cut them out of me," I groan.

"I don't think that's right," Sophie replies, not getting that I'm exaggerating. Or am I? By now, I don't care what way these creatures leave my body, as long as they're gone.

She lifts her knife. "It's not sharp enough anyway. Do you need me to find my father? Can he help you?"

I glare at her. "No, I don't want him to help me. I want him dead."

She blinks. She shouldn't be surprised at that. "Okay. I'll do it."

She runs off before I can stop her. I groan, unable to even get to my feet. I need to get to her before she makes a mistake. She's not strong enough to face him. Nor do I want her to become a killer.

Something sharp pushes against my cervix. Please, not claws. I have no idea how my babies will look, if they'll be born as humans or shifted, but I really hope no claws will be involved. I know that kittens can't sheathe their claws when they're born, so if I'm unlucky - and I've been unlucky a lot recently - I might end up with a torn vagina.

I'm going to kill Delaney as soon as my uterus is empty again. I wish I could give him the pain I'm going through, but sadly, men just aren't made for this. No surprise. They'd probably be dead by now.

I wish I was, too. I scream as I'm torn into pieces.

"Breathe, Kat, breathe."

Gryphon is suddenly by my side. The pain has dulled my senses and I never even heard him approach. Him being here rather than fighting is a good sign.

"I'll breathe when they're out," I groan. "Just pull them out for me."

"That's now how it works. Lie on your back, I'll check how far you are."

"Not happening. I'm more comfortable on all fours."

"That's fine. I dimly remember from my training that the pregnant woman is in charge."

"You bet. Not just when she's pregnant."

He chuckles just when another wave of agony threatens to drown me.

"Is everyone alright?" I pant once I surface. The pain is

still there, still burning through me, but it's a tiny bit less than during the contraction.

"Ryker and Lennox are dealing with the last of the mutants. I've not seen Sophie anywhere."

"She went after Delaney. Go stop her. I-"

My sentence ends in a scream.

"Breathe."

I'm ready to knife him if he says that word one more time.

"Make sure Sophie's alright. Please."

He strokes my hair back, mixing blood with sweat, then nods and runs off. I'm glad he's listening to me. Now that he's gone, I can let go of all control again and cry out the pain as much as I want. I don't have to pretend it's not as awful as it is.

With every contraction, I grow weaker. My body still hasn't recovered from my imprisonment and it shows. I want to shift so bad, but I know that's a bad idea. All I can hope for is that it will be over soon.

I can barely hold myself up on all fours. Maybe I should roll on my back after all, but even the thought of that makes me break out in sweat.

Another contraction and the world swirls around me. Bile rises in my throat as vertigo takes a hold of my body. I no longer know what's up and what's down. I turn, trying to follow gravity, but I end up on my side, I think. It's confusing.

I spread my legs wide when something pushes from inside and suddenly, it all goes very fast. With more pain than I thought possible, a slimy, heavy object slips out of me, right into Lennox's waiting hands. I no longer scream. I'm drifting, barely registering what's happening. It's like I'm a passerby, watching the scene from afar. The second baby is caught by Ryker. They came back to me just in time. And then there's Gryphon, telling me stuff I can't hear, expertly cutting the umbilical cords.

Pressure builds up in me again. Two more to go. I think they're fighting for who gets to leave my uterus first, judging from the searing pain.

Sophie comes running with towels; they must be from the pub we stayed in. Gryphon helps the third baby into the world. I watch impassively at the bloody little being. I should probably feel something for the three tiny parasites being held by my men, but I don't. I'm numb, ready to go to sleep.

The last one almost slips out too fast, taking the slide its siblings have created. I think my insides are a mess and let's not even think about my vagina. A pussy with a broken pussy.

Now that they're all out, the pain gets less, enough for me to close my eyes and let myself fall into blissful, warm unconsciousness.

CHAPTER TWO

The next five days pass in a haze. I lie on a blanket the guys have spread over several bales of straw, wishing we were home already. The wagon they've taken from the pub is making our journey slower than on horseback, but there's no way I could ride. Blood still pours from between my legs and the guys have to replace the towels every hour or so. If I wasn't a shifter, I'd be dead by now. My body is trying to heal itself, but it's barely keeping up with the damage the babies have wrought within me.

Sophie and Gryphon are by my side while Lennox is driving the wagon. Ryker is on a horse, scouting ahead and making sure we're not being followed.

Delaney escaped the battle. On one hand, I'm glad because it means I still get to kill him, but on the other hand, it complicates everything. We're still in danger. I bet those weren't his only mutant guards. He'll get more and he'll come after us. And when he does, I won't be able to defend myself or my family.

The day after giving birth, my breasts started leaking milk. I was both relieved and horrified. Four days later and my nipples look like they've been mauled by beasts. Which comes pretty close to the truth.

Because I'm too weak to even lift the babies, Gryphon or Sophie hold them in place while they torture me. Neither humans nor cats should be born with teeth, but my litter didn't get that message. They all look human at first glance, but it's clear they're more than that. Two have the golden eyes of my panther and tiny fangs. They look completely alike, although to be fair, to me all babies look the same, so it's too early to say if that'll still be the case once they get older. The third baby has a soft layer of fur all over its body, making her resemble an ape. And finally, the only male, who's completely human from the front - until you realise he's got a tail. Yes, my baby has a tail.

We've not given them names yet. It's been too quick, too overwhelming. For now, all they do is feed, sleep and scream. When they're not torturing my nipples and sucking me dry like tiny vampires, they're either sleeping by my side or snuggled into slings the guys have wrapped around their chests.

Even in my daze, I can appreciate how hot my males look with babies on them. All three guys have taken to them instantly and the adoring and protective looks they give them almost make me jealous. Sophie treats my litter like an older sister rather than an aunt. To be fair, she's closer to them in age than to me, so it makes sense.

I don't know what I feel when I look at them. It's not the love I feel for my males. Not what I have for Sophie either, although I can't quite identify that emotion either. Yet when I imagine anything happening to them, my heart hurts almost as much as my womb did when I gave birth to them. My fingers itch as my claws threaten to burst to the surface. Yes, I'm fiercely protective of my litter. Does that mean I love them?

I cling to the hope that everything will become clear once we reach our home. I can't wait to be back in my hammock. To see my sister, Lily and the others. It's been way too long. I need a break, some time with them, before I can start planning my revenge. A growl escapes me. They're going to suffer. Delaney, his wife, any siren I can get my hands on.

The cart creaks as we drive over some uneven, stony ground. Lennox looks back apologetically, but it's not like he can do anything about the state of the roads. They'll get better once we get closer to Attenburgh. Here, the local farmers don't have money to keep up the roads and I doubt the government helps with it either. Luckily, Lady Lara spends her money wisely and has worked on improving the main trading routes into the city.

I miss my conversations with her. When I was self-kidnapped - no, *kidnapped*, I need to stop thinking of it as anything else - I'd only just made up with her. I'd planned to work for her again, this time not as a bodyguard but as an adviser. I'm not sure I'd be good at it, but I love a challenge. Besides, working alongside Lady Lara is a treat. She's intelligent, down to earth and reliable. Plus, she has a naughty streak hidden deep inside of her. Until I discovered that she'd planned to have the best thieves in the town eaten by monstrous fish, I would never have expected her to be this similar to me. Although it's safe to say that I wouldn't have failed in giving those fish their dinner.

"Want to play a game?" Sophie asks, way cheerier than I feel. "I spy with my little eye?"

I let my gaze wander over the dreary landscape. Fields, the occasional tree, lots of mud. Thick grey clouds warn of yet more rain. Nothing that stands out. We're the only specks of colour on an otherwise depressingly grey canvas.

"There must be a better game we can play," I sigh. "Give me that yellow flower and I'll show you one."

At our last stop, Sophie picked a whole bunch of flowers. I don't know what any of them called; I'd only know that if they were poisonous and therefore part of my assassin's repertoire.

She hands me the flower and I run my finger over its soft petals. They're already starting to wither, so what I'm about to do is a mercy.

"Kill." I pluck a petal and let it drift to the bottom of the cart. "Maim." Another petal. "Kill. Maim. Kill. Maim."

I grin at Sophie, but she doesn't seem to get that this game is fun.

"Are you thinking of someone when you do that?" she asks.

I nod. "I do. It's far more satisfying this way."
"Who?"

Should I tell her it's her father? I know she's no longer under his control, but I doubt she's ready to hear my plans for torturing him slowly, very slowly, taking him apart limb by limb.

"Someone who hurt me," I say instead. "And those who're important to me."

"That's good then," she replies, once again sounding older than she is. "I can help you."

I'm both proud of her and a little sad. Just like the twins, she's been exposed to way more violence than children should. I've managed to give the twins a new life, so hopefully, I'll be able to do the same for Sophie. I don't want her to become a ruthless assassin. She's got a sweet, gentle side that I've come to notice in the past few days. The way she holds her nieces and nephew speaks of a loving heart that I would hate to witness breaking.

She takes a flower with blue petals that turn a dark purple towards the edges and starts muttering "kill, maim".

"Who are you thinking of?" I ask her with an amused smirk.

"Jagger, one of the men who guarded our house. He wasn't nice to me."

"Good girl. We'll get to him, don't worry. I'll kill him for you."

"Or maim him," she insists. "I'm not done yet."

I watch her patiently as she removes the petals one by one, ending with a triumphant "kill". I got the same result for my flower. Looks like there's going to be a lot of death in my near future.

"I'd need an entire field of flowers," Gryphon says loudly against the rattling of the cart and takes my hand. "My list has grown fast in the past few months. So many people who didn't want to tell me what they knew. I already got rid of some of them, but I didn't always have the time to stick around."

One day, I'm going to ask them to tell me everything that happened to them while they searched for me. But not now. My hormones are still all over the place and I'd likely end up emotional. I don't want to risk it.

"Are you comfortable back there?" Lennox asks, turning around to look at me. He's been doing that every hour or so. It's both sweet and extremely annoying.

"The cart is still as bumpy as it was two hours ago," I reply drily. "But it is what it is. Will we reach Attenburgh tomorrow?"

He nods. "If those clouds don't drop any rain, then yes. If it rains, we'll need an extra day; the ground is still soaked from this week's downpours and if any more water is added, it'll turn into a river of mud."

I wish I could ride, but that's a silly fantasy in my current state. I should be glad that we have this cart, but it's hard to be optimistic when your entire body hurts, especially those nipples. Now I know why some mothers don't breastfeed their offspring. If I had milk and bottles, I may do the same, especially with four of them. I doubt I'll ever be able to produce enough milk, especially once they grow and need even more.

Attenburgh can't come soon enough. I'm going to get Bethany to create some fake breast milk for my babies. If she can do poisons that can slowly melt a human's skin from the inside, she can make sustenance for tiny shifters.

If they are shifters. So far, they've all stayed human, but none of us has any experience with baby shifters. The children brought to the Pack were usually at least three or four. By that age, they sometimes shifted by accident, which is why everyone was given a collar at arrival, no matter the age. I have no idea if my babies are capable of shifting and I don't have anyone to ask. Neither does Lennox; we're both orphans.

Sophie can't remember when she was first able to shift, so she's no help either. When we're in Attenburgh, we'll be able to call Lennox's ex-boss, Mister Moon, who may have some answers for us. Someone in his group of werewolves has to know when shifter babies first start changing shape. I hope it doesn't happen while they're suckling on my boobs. That would end painfully. It's already bad enough that two of the girls have fangs. I look down at my chest. It's not a pretty sight beneath my shirt.

"I'm bored," Sophie huffs. "Can't we play I spy now?"

I roll my eyes. Guess I won't get a nap anytime soon.

CHAPTER THREE

I'm bleeding again by the time we roll into Attenburgh. I'm trying to stay awake despite the blood pouring from between my legs, but it's only because I'm excited about finally being back home that I'm managing to stay conscious. Both Gryphon and Ryker are on the cart with me, while Sophie is sitting next to Lennox. He's letting her steer the cart, but I know he's ready to pick up the reins at any moment in case she gets distracted again.

"Not much longer," Gryphon mutters and runs a cool hand over my forehead. "As soon as we've got you home, I'll be able to help you properly."

I squeeze his hand. "You've done what you could."

He grimaces but doesn't reply. No matter how often I tell him that nobody could have done more than he has with limited supply and tools, he still blames himself for failing to heal me. It's silly and I've told him exactly that. There's only room for so much self-pity on this cart and the majority of it is my own. And I'm allowed to wallow in self-pity, especially when my fanged babies start mauling my boobs.

Luckily, they're all asleep. They fed an hour ago, which usually makes them sleepy enough to give us all some rest. They're curled up in a heap in their basket. The little male is sucking on the thumb of one of his sisters. I smile with adoration before drawing the blanket over the basket to hide them from the view of curious onlookers. At first glance, they look like human babies, but I don't want anyone to give them a second look and notice the fangs, tail and fur.

We're making slow progress now that we're on busy streets rather than the empty, bumpy roads we've grown used to. Humans mill all around us, going about their business, but most don't pay us any heed. We're just one cart amongst many others that are entering Attenburgh. Most are headed to the market, but not us. Our house in on the outskirts, but annoyingly not in the direction we came from. We could have circled the city, but in the end, we decided to drive right through in the hope that this might be faster.

This morning, we passed a little hamlet where Gryphon was able to call Lily, announcing our pending arrival. I don't know what he told her, but I bet she's going to be prepared with medical supplies in the hope of finally fixing me.

A new wave of pain racks through my abdomen and I wrap my hands around my belly, riding the pain. At least the bump has gone and I can see my feet again. While my insides are still injured, the outside has healed fast and there's no trace left of my pregnancy. My stomach is nice and tight again, no flabbiness anywhere to be seen. Still, if I could swap having a bump against not bleeding out from inside, I'd do that without hesitation. I'm not that vain.

"That's the house we stayed in," Sophie suddenly shouts, pointing at a large villa. It must belong to Delaney.

I exchange a grim look with my guys and they nod in understanding. As soon as I'm better, we'll raid that place and torch it to the ground. Any asset that could give Delaney an advantage has to be destroyed. From now on, I'm not waiting for him to come after me. I'm going on the offensive and I won't stop until he and every single evil siren in this country has been vanquished.

We drive on in silence. When we leave the main roads and turn onto narrower streets, Lennox takes the reins from Sophie. She complains a little, but she respects him enough not to throw a tantrum. She has a lot more respect for my males than she has for me, probably because all the crap Delaney and his wife told her about me.

I look around us as if it's the first time I'm driving through the city. It feels like an eternity since I was last here. So much has changed since then. I'm no longer the same.

When we finally reach our house, I sigh in relief. My pain has become a steady throb and the cloth between my legs is soaked with blood. I don't think I'll be able to walk into our home. I cringe at the thought of having to be carried yet again. I hate being weak, even though my guys reassure me constantly that they love taking care of me. It must satisfy some kind of alpha instinct in them, especially in Lennox. His wolf chose me as his mate and it's only because of Lennox's cool-headed personality that he accepted that he'd have to share me. The wolf would never have agreed to that, but luckily, Lennox is a shifter who's learned to be in control of his animal instincts. I guess I have the Pack to thank for that.

The door flies open as soon as we stop in front of the M.E.O.W. headquarters and Lily runs out, closely followed by Bethany and Benjamin. They must have been waiting for us.

"Kat!" Lily yells and faster than I thought possible for an almost-human, she's on the cart, by my side, looking down at me with concern. "How are you?"

I try to smile but I'm pretty sure it looks more like a tense grimace. "I'll be fine."

She raises her eyebrows, clearly spotting the lie, then turns to Gryphon. "I've turned the morgue into an operating theatre with everything you requested. The mayor has sent a surgeon who apparently knows how to keep her mouth shut. And Bethany has prepared various potions and salves that might help."

He shoots her a grateful smile. A strange acidic taste spreads in my mouth. He shouldn't smile at her like that. Wait, am I jealous? It must be the blood loss that is messing with my emotions.

They carry me into the house like an invalid while Benjamin runs ahead to open all the doors. I start laughing when we go downstairs into the morgue. Never thought I'd end up in there. At least not while I'm still alive.

"What's wrong?" Gryphon asks with perfectly cute concern.

"Morgue," I say. "Kind of morbid."

He rolls his eyes. "Only you would laugh about that."

From behind us, Ryker chuckles. "Not just her. You have to admit, it's kind of strange to take her into the morgue to fix her. That's not normal."

"Since when are we normal?" Lennox quips. "I take that as an insult."

In the morgue, they lay me on the metal table where we usually dissect corpses. Fun. I hope they remember that unlike the dead, I still feel pain and need anaesthetics if they start operating on me. Gryphon said he won't know what to do until he's had a proper look at what's wrong inside of me.

A small, wiry woman stands in one corner, gaping at us with wide eyes. That must be the surgeon the mayor organised.

While Gryphon starts talking to her, the other guys fuss over me, trying to make me more comfortable on the cold table. A mattress beneath me would have been nice, but I know that wouldn't have been hygienic. I'll survive without it…I hope.

Bethany takes various bottles from a shelf and arranges them on a trolley. With Lily standing in the doorway, the room is way too cramped. Gryphon must have realised the same thing.

"Everyone not essential, get out."

Nobody moves.

He sighs. "Yes, you're all essential, but we don't need you all here. Lily, why don't you help Sophie with the babies and show her around. Lennox, call the mayor and let her know we've returned. Ryker, I'm sure we could use some food once we're done here."

"I've already prepared a nursery," Lily says cheerfully. "Including two scratch posts."

She dances away, clearly ecstatic at the thought of playing with my babies.

Lennox glares at Gryphon, but then presses a kiss on my forehead and leaves, followed by Ryker, whose kiss meets my lips. Tease. As soon as I can move without losing blood again, I'm going to show them all how much I've hated being babied by them. The image of handcuffs and leashes flashes into my mind and I grin evilly.

"This is Doctor Lavalle," Gryphon introduces the small woman. She gives me a small smile but it doesn't reach her eyes. "She's going to start with an ultrasound while I give you something for the pain. If we have to operate, we'll sedate you, but for now, just some analgesics to take the edge off."

They spring into action and I let them do whatever needs doing. Bethany, done with her preparations, comes to stand at the end of the table, looking down at me with a grin.

"It's good to have you back. It was boring without you."

"Glad I'll be able to stop the boredom," I say drily. "Did nothing interesting happen while I was away?"

"Ryker's cats tamed the deer, Willow. They use her to ride on and get up to all sorts of mischief. I'm convinced they can talk to each other, even though Ryker said that's impossible."

"I thought the fawn would be gone by now."

Bethany laughs. "Benjamin would have left along with it. He loves Willow even more than he loves the cats. They're inseparable. She sleeps on his bed and follows him everywhere – unless the cats have kidnapped her for their evil plans."

I can't wait to see that. I almost forgot about the fawn I rescued. It feels like years ago. I assumed Benjamin would release it into the wild as soon as it was fully grown, but it seems like I was wrong. I should have known. Benjamin gets attached to animals. It's kind of sweet. I suppose he got attached to M.E.O.W. too. In the beginning, I thought he'd move on as soon as he'd earned some money, but here he is, still part of our little team. Well, no longer that little. If this growth continues, I may have to consider paying taxes at some point. No. Not happening. As much as I like Lady Lara, I'm an assassin and criminals don't pay taxes as a rule. Maybe I could donate a statue or something silly like that to make up for it. An animal rescue that can deal with the strays Ryker can't look after.

"We're going to have to operate," Doctor Lavalle says, sounding very grave. "It's a miracle you're still alive."

I don't know how much she knows about me, so I keep my mouth shut.

"How long is it going to take?" Bethany asks.

"Hard to say until we open her up and see the state of things. Three hours at the very least, depending on how skilled this young man is."

She nods towards Gryphon. He looks a little offended but doesn't protest. It's true that he never finished his medical studies, but he's got a lot of practical experience. I doubt I'd have survived childbirth without him.

I close my eyes and try to relax. The pain is making that rather hard, but hopefully, it'll be gone soon.

"You better get on with it," I mutter and grit my teeth. "And if I don't wake up, I'm going to haunt you for the rest of your lives."

CHAPTER FOUR

ONE MONTH LATER

"Y**ou *cannot* call your daughter Catnip," Lily groans and rolls her eyes. "She'll never forgive you for that."

"It's a perfectly decent name. Lady Lara's secretary is called Apple. If a human can call her daughter after food, so can I."

"And what about the others? String? Milk? Mouse?"

"Mouse is rather nice," I say innocently, even though I'm starting to see her point.

Today, we're having a naming ceremony for my litter. Until now, I've called them Tailie, Vamp, Biter and Furrie, but I know they can't keep those names, as cute as they are. For now, the four of them are behaving like regular human babies, if you ignore the fangs and an unusually fast developing dexterity. Tailie keeps wrapping his tiny tail around my arm when I carry him, reminding me of a monkey. He's got a surprising control of it already. They're growing as slowly as human babies, but they're already able to sit on their own and turn onto their bellies. Soon, they'll start to crawl and all hell will break loose.

"Maybe you should stick with the C-theme," Lily suggests. "Cara, Cain, Claudia, Caramel."

"Caramel is food too. I thought you didn't like food-related names."

"Cindy then. Those are normal names."

"And boring ones," I sigh.

I've already had this conversation with the guys and we ended up with an endless list of names, but not a single one of them felt right to me. My babies aren't ordinary. They need names that show how special they really are.

"Fury," I mutter thoughtfully. "Vengeance. Justice. Wrath."

"You can't be serious."

I shoot her a stern look. "I am."

"You have three males, why not let them name one girl each and you name the boy? That way you can make them feel even more involved in their care."

I roll my eyes. "Some days I feel they're more involved in their lives than I am. Take now, I'm here with you while Ryker and Gryphon are playing with the litter. Lennox is researching shifter babies. And even Bethany is part of it all, trying to synthesise my breast milk."

"And Benjamin is out shopping for the nursery," Lily interrupts. "We're all trying to help. You have four babies; you can't be expected to do everything yourself. Besides, it's not like you chose to get pregnant."

I shudder. I hate it when someone mentions that. I want to forget where my offspring came from. All I want to do is focus on the present and on their future. The past is gone. There's nothing I can do about it.

"What else is he getting?" I ask. "That room is full enough already."

Lily shrugs. "No idea. Maybe a new mobile after Tailie pulled it down with his tail and the others destroyed it."

I laugh at the memory of seeing the four of them surrounded by carnage, proudly looking up at me, expecting praise for tearing apart their mobile. I doubt human babies would have been able to do that. For now, none of them has claws, but I doubt it'll stay that way. Vamp already moves her hands as if her fingernails were longer than they are.

Back when I was pregnant, Gryphon used his siren senses to find out what my babies were. He thought that two of them were cat shifters and two of them sirens mixed with shifter genes, one of them a wolf and one something he couldn't identify.

I'm starting to think he was wrong. I think they're all cat shifters. Vamp and Bitie clearly have a cat's fangs and Tailie's tail is feline too. Furrie's body hair could be a number of animals, but she behaves the same way as the others. Now that they've been born, I'm wondering more and more who their father is. Are they the products of genetic experiments?. What if they're Delaney's biological children? What if he implanted me with his seed while I was imprisoned?

I shudder at the thought and clench my hands. It's much easier to think that they did some scientific experiments on me than the alternative. I'm used to being experimented on; it's happened to me all my life.

Once I get Delaney into my claws, I'll get a sample of his blood to do a paternity test. I need to know, even though I'm not sure how I'd cope with the truth. Either way, I'll never tell them how they were conceived. I want them to feel wanted and loved, as if I'd planned to have them.

I sense Ryker moments before he storms into the room.

"Someone's arrived at the villa," he announces with barely withheld excitement. "My cats saw two people enter. It could be Delaney."

I'm on my feet instantly, already buzzing with blood lust. We've been waiting for this moment. Torching the house with nobody inside didn't seem right. I also needed time to heal, but now that I'm back to full health, this is the perfect opportunity to see if my skills are still what they used to be. Besides some walks on the city's rooftops by night and one tiny assassination, I've not gone back to my old job yet. I'm sure the house is being watched and I didn't want any of Delaney's cronies to see that I'm still alive – and returning to my old self. It's taken two weeks to regain weight and muscle and the other two weeks have been full of suckling babies and boring admin stuff. Now though, I'm itching to get active and do something messier than changing diapers.

Lily gets up and shoots me an indulgent smile. "I'll look after the babies, you go and have fun. Shall I tell Lennox and Gryphon to join you there?"

"Lennox already knows," Ryker says with barely withheld impatience. "He'll come as soon as you or one of the others takes over babysitting."

I'm already out of the room, grabbing weapons from the coat rack by the door. We've turned it into a mini armoury with a few of everyone's favourite weapons, for emergencies. We also have an entire room full of toys, everything from knives to crossbows to smoke bombs, but I don't have time to go there. I already have a knife in each boot plus my trusty poison darts in my shirt collar. I never go anywhere without them. I've had to make sure that they can't accidentally sting the babies when they clumsily grab my shirt, but that was easily solved with tiny plastic sheaths, no larger than a matchstick each.

"Are you going to shift?" I ask Ryker when he joins me.

"No, I'm in the mood for slashing something." He grins evilly. While I was away, he trained with the others, improving his weapon skills. For someone who couldn't even walk upright a year ago, he's made excellent progress. Having lived all his life as a cat has given him excellent balance and reaction speed. He keeps saying that he wants to make himself some gloves with blades at the fingertips like claws, but he's not turned that idea into reality yet.

We run, taking back alleys and a couple of detours to stay out of sight of humans. It's broad daylight and I don't want us to draw attention before we've even reached the villa. Once we're there, that's a different matter. I can't wait to sink my blades into something fleshy.

By the time we get to the house, I'm breathing way faster than I should be. I thought I was fully recovered but it seems I'm not as far as I'd hoped. I need to build up stamina again. Luckily, that gives me an excuse to get out of the house despite everyone's concerns that I may be seen. After today, Delaney will know that I'm still alive. I hope he's here, ready to be killed.

Three cats await us in a cul-de-sac behind the villa. I don't recognise any of them, but I immediately take to the black female with beautiful golden eyes. She's a miniature me. I know some humans have superstitions about black cats, but that's only because we're so amazing. They're scared of us. I bet even this small kitty could take down a human, if she really put her mind to it.

"Has anyone left the building since you alerted us?" Ryker asks.

The largest of the cats, an elegant Sphynx that could do with some fur, shakes her head. Ryker has taught them basic gestures likes that and nodding to make it easier to communicate with us when we're not shifted. I wonder if he's added to their motion vocabulary while I was gone. Something to explore later.

Ryker holds out a hand and grins at me. "My lady, shall we go?"

"Are you inviting me on a date?"

"Indeed I am. I must warn you, though, there may be blood. I hope the lady won't faint at the sight?"

I manage a ladylike giggle. "If I do, you'll have to catch me in your strong, muscular arms."

"You have yourself a deal. And I may keep you in my arms once I've caught you. I can't guarantee you'll keep your clothes on, either."

The black cat meows. I feel like she'd roll her eyes if she could.

I look up at the house and let the humour drain away, putting on my assassin mask. The time for joking over. The time for vengeance has arrived.

WE ENTER THROUGH A FIRE ESCAPE AT THE BACK. A complete security oversight, if you ask me, but I doubt Delaney will want my opinion. The door at the top of the ladder is locked and most likely alarmed, but now that we're here, I no longer care about subterfuge. I don't want to murder Delaney from behind. I want him to look me in the face while I slowly, painfully take his life.

If he's even there. I mentally cross my fingers. This would make it nice and easy. Kill Delaney, then concentrate on eliminating his allies. Could the Great Cat in the Sky smile on me just this once? I think I've earned a little luck.

Ryker looks at me, his expression hard. "Ready?"

I nod. "Let's do this. You go downstairs and block the door; we don't want any escaping. I'll find Delaney if he's here."

"Alright, but only until the others arrive. I'll join you as soon as they're here. I've got my own bill to settle with that fucking siren."

His body is tense with barely withheld anger, surprising me. I thought I was the only one keen to dismember and decapitate Delaney.

"What bill?" I ask, feeling like I should know the answer myself.

Ryker stares at me. "Really? You think it was easy for me when you were gone? You think I – we – don't hate the siren just as much as you? You were the one who was tortured by him, but trust me, it feels like he inflicted the same pain on me. On my heart. Not knowing where you were, if you were even still alive, it killed me inside. The guys and I have just as much reason to want to kill him as you."

"But-"

"No buts. This isn't just about you. It's about all of us, our family. Choosing us all means more than just having three men to fuck. We're in this together, and I know it's hard, you're not used to having people who love you, but you need to get used to it. Fast. We've given you time to recover, but I don't think we can wait much longer. You need to open up, tell us what happened. We can only help if we know everything."

I gape at him. I didn't expect this, not in the slightest. I had no idea. Am I really this clueless? Did I miss all the signs of the guys being unhappy? Is that even it?

"Are you unhappy?" I whisper, my assassin mask crumbling away. Fuck. This isn't the time for personal baggage, but we probably have to discuss this now that we've started, or neither of us will be able to focus fully on the task at hand.

He slowly shakes his head. "No, not unhappy. Just… I don't even know. I guess I want to feel like I'm needed. Not just for looking after your litter. I want to listen to your problems and I want to solve them. I want to be there for you emotionally, not just physically, but for that, you need to let me in. You can't keep us out forever, Kat. It's not fair. We're ready to bare ourselves to you, but it has to go both ways."

Bare myself. Let down my guards. I'd started doing that, before I was kidnapped. But now, I don't think I can. I'm a mess inside. I'm not sure I'll ever be the same again. Delaney broke me, even though I'd never admit that. He crushed me into pieces and the babies are a constant reminder of that. I love them, but every time I look at them, those shards of ugly memories cut into my heart.

"I know you're not alright yet, Kat," he says softly. "You don't have to pretend that you are. When we're back home, we're going to talk about it. No excuses. We're going to lock ourselves into a room and we're not going to leave it until everything's been discussed."

A shiver runs down my back. I don't think I can do this. The thought of it makes me more scared than I am of being back in that cell.

"You didn't choose the best time to discuss this," I say with a fake laugh.

"No, probably not." He gives me a small smile, but I know he's not ready to drop the topic. "But I've not had the chance to be alone with you since you got back. I guess I couldn't put it off any longer. Sorry."

"You have nothing to be sorry for." I mean it. I get

where he's coming from. I just wish it were all a little easier.

I take a deep breath. "Shall we kill a siren?"

His smile gives way to a flash of his teeth. "With pleasure."

CHAPTER FIVE

As soon as we open the door, a shrill alarm starts blaring through the house. I cringe at the noise, but I bet the switch to turn it off is downstairs by the main door, the way it always is. I've dealt with enough security systems to know the standards. Ryker winks at me, all back to his normal, jovial self, and runs off towards the large staircase at the end of the corridor we've entered. Before we opened the door, I'd extended my senses and felt for whoever is in the house. Five people. I couldn't discern whether they're siren, human or otherwise; the walls are too thick to give me their scents so I have to go by heartbeat alone. Five. I was hoping for more. Hopefully, the others won't arrive until it's all over, that will leave more killing for me.

Two of the people are downstairs, to be dealt with by Ryker, two are on my level and one's above me. I rely on my instincts and decide to head upstairs. Hopefully, that person is Delaney, alone in his office.

My blades are in my hands, ready to throw or slash, whatever's necessary. The adrenaline coursing through me is a welcome change from all the dullness of the past weeks. Not that looking after four babies is boring, but I've missed this. My senses are on full alert and the world seems sharper. I notice everything, from the tiny dead spider on the floor, half-hidden by clouds of dust, to the yellowish stains on the ceiling that talk of past water damage.

I doubt this house is used very often. Sophie said her father took her here only once, when he forced me to turn into his prisoner. The smell of mothballs permeates the air, along with the stale dryness that tells of a home that isn't aired often enough. I can almost taste the dust, even though my careful footsteps don't cause any to be flung into the air.

Below me, a fight has started. I don't have any doubts that Ryker can deal with the two people, even if they're mutants. He's got the reflexes of a cat and will dance around them, never letting their weapons close.

It's strange that the two people on this floor haven't moved at all, despite the alarm that is still blaring through the air. I've managed to block it out, but it prevents me from listening to any conversations that may be going on. It's likely that Delaney – or whoever else is in charge – will have called backup by now.

Logic dictates I should deal with this floor first, but the hate for the siren makes me run up the staircase instead. This level has an entirely different feel to it. Dark cherry wood covers the walls, making it look both older and more luxurious. The air smells of cigar smoke. Not something I ever noticed in the house I was held prisoner in, but then, I never progressed to Delaney's living quarters. Maybe it's his vice. Maybe he sits in his office, surrounded by smoke, coming up with his evil plans while sipping on a glass of whisky. I wouldn't put it past him. It would match his perfect suits, the politician persona. A smooth, polished businessman with a black, evil heart underneath the fake smile.

Finally, the alarm stops, leaving only blissful silence. That must be Ryker's doing. I breathe in deep, urging my ears to stop ringing. I zone in on the heartbeat on this floor, straight ahead from me. I ignore all the other doors, although I'm a little jealous of their polished golden doorknobs. Maybe I should steal some on the way out; they'd look great in my own house.

I hesitate in front of the final door. The wood here is carved into something that looks like poison ivy. How fitting. I'm sure at least two of my darts are dipped into a mixture that includes ivy. The darts are a last resort though in case this goes pear-shaped. I want to torture Delaney first, slowly peeling down his barriers, exposing his insides, before looking him straight into the eyes as his life extinguishes. I lick my lips at the image. It's going to feel good.

The heartbeat inside the room sounds familiar, but I've not been around Delaney often enough to know for sure if it's him. Only one way to find out.

I tighten my fingers around my knives. It's time to face my demons.

The person behinds the desk doesn't move when I barge into the room. She smiles, seemingly relaxed, as she takes me in.

"I was wondering if it will be you."

Delaney's wife is dressed in a pale blue costume with a high collar. Her perfectly styled hair falls onto her shoulders in even, dark-brown curls. Her eyes, too far apart to count as beautiful, are cold and calculating. She smells of rose perfume and siren. Most of that scent probably comes from her husband, but I could imagine that she's got some siren blood herself. She's not pretty enough to be a full siren, but I somehow doubt that someone like Lord Delaney would take a mere human as his wife.

"Where's your husband?" I bark.

"Not here, obviously. You'll have to deal with me. But you better hurry, we've got guards on the way."

I roll my eyes. "As if they could stop me. Are you ready to die, Gill?"

I found out her first name during the research we did on the Delaney family in the past few weeks. It was easy to find out general information on them, especially on Gill's husband and his political work, but I don't know much about their personal life besides dates when they got married and such like.

"I'm not the one who's going to die today." Her face stays impassive, but the flicker of fear in her eyes is hard to miss.

"If you tell me where your husband is, I might make it quick. Or we could draw it out. After what you did to me, I'm in the mood for retribution. Do you want to know what it feels like to lie on a scorching-hot floor? Would you like to be starved? I'm sure I could create a little cell for you in my own basement. Give you some of your own medicine, so to speak."

"You're crazy. You have no idea what's going to happen. If you want to stay alive, run now, far away. We know where you live. We know who your little friends are. It's only because we've been too busy with more important things that you're still alive. In a week, this country is going to change for the better. We're going to get rid of your kind, once and for all. A few of you will stay in our labs, but we won't tolerate feral animals running around, pretending to be humans."

All fear has been extinguished and is now replaced by hate. I wonder where that hate for shifters has come from.

She raised a cat shifter as her daughter – does she hate Sophie as well? I'd hoped there may have been at least a flicker of love or affection towards my little sister.

I grin at her, swirling my knives in my hands. "Thanks for telling me your plans. Now you just have to point me to wherever your husband is hiding and I'll be on my way."

With her as a corpse on the floor, obviously. I won't let her live.

"Anything else you want to tell me?" I ask her. "Last chance."

Shouts come from below me, followed by a loud crash.

"Time's up," I say, almost regretful that I haven't been able to torture the woman. I won't regret her death, though. It was on my to-do list ever since she visited me in that cell.

"You don't want to do this," she says, a tiny waver in her voice. Her hands move to a drawer beneath her desk, probably for a weapon.

You look pathetic, she told me back when I first met her.

Before she can use whatever's in the drawer, I fling my knife at her, hitting her straight in her right eye.

"You're pathetic," I say out loud while she slowly slides to one side, her body shutting down.

By the time she falls off her chair and hits the floor, she's dead.

I check the drawer. A tiny crossbow with a single arrow. I give it a sniff. It's not even poisoned.

"Pathetic," I repeat and run out of the room, ready to help Ryker and do some proper killing.

* * * * * *

HE'S SURROUNDED BY BODIES, GRINNING LIKE A MANIAC AND covered in blood. Just the way I like him. He turns to greet me just when one of the grunts behind him gets back to his feet. One of those immortal ones. Without taking his eyes off me, Ryker flings the long blade he's holding and throws it at the man. It embeds itself between the mutant's eyes and he falls backwards, a comically surprised expression on his brutish face.

"Nice one," I praise Ryker. "You really have learned a lot while I was gone."

He grins proudly. "I realised I need to rely more on my feline instincts, even when human. It helps me see things with more than just my eyes."

I do a quick count of the bodies. Seven. Respect for Ryker fills me. Even I would have struggled to take on that many grunts. He's cut off the heads of most of them, but there's one he forgot. Or maybe he was a gentleman and saved that one for me.

He hands me his blade, longer than my knives and more suited for the job, then I get to work. I do love a good beheading, although it's more fun to do it while the target is still alive. This is more like woodcutting.

"There are still two people on the floor above us," he says once I'm done. "They've not moved at all."

"No sign of the others yet?"

"Nope, but it's not like we needed them. Lennox will be pissed that he missed all the action; he's been craving a good fight."

"It wasn't Lord Delaney up there, just his wife. This isn't the end of it, there will be many more fights, if I'm not mistaken." I sigh. "As much as I want to take revenge, I can't wait until it's all over and we get to spend some family time together."

He raises an eyebrow, pretending to be shocked. "Who are you and what did you do to Kat? Family time? Did I just hear that correctly?"

I punch his shoulder. "Don't tell anyone I said that."

"Not a word. But I get you. The last few months have been exhausting for all of us. Well, every single day since I met you. Not that I regret it." He pulls me close and presses my lips against mine. He smells of blood, sweat and catnip; the best smell in the world.

I kiss him back, soaking in the comfort he's giving me. We're surrounded by carnage, yet I wouldn't want to be anywhere else. Ryker's kiss is home; a place I never want to leave.

His arousal is hardening against my belly, but as much as I would like to give in to the urge to rip off our clothes and take him here and now, this isn't the time nor place.

With more regret than I thought I could feel, I swipe my tongue against his front teeth one last time before stepping back.

"Later?" he asks breathlessly.

"Later. Let's check out those two people above."

He nods, all softness leaving his expression. I also don my assassin mantle, ignoring the remnants of desire pulsing through my veins. We can continue that kiss – and more – once we're back home.

We walk upstairs without making a sound. The thick carpet lining the stairs helps with that. The blood will be awful to get out of it though. We're leaving bloody footprints, but I don't care, both our friends and our enemies would be able to find us without them.

The closer we get to the two people, the more I feel like something's off. Their heartbeats are too slow, as if they're sleeping. There's no way though that anyone slept through the racket Ryker made when he took on seven grunts.

He shoots me a look when we reach the door behind which I can sense the mysterious people.

I nod to show that I'm ready. Ryker reaches for the

doorknob just when a strange scent hits my nostrils. I act out of instinct, pushing against him with all my might, causing us to tumble to the ground. I land on top of him, my knee between his legs. Oops.

"What the fuck was that for?" he groans, clutching his crotch.

"Poison," I huff and jump to my feet, holding out a hand. He grips it and I pull him up.

He sniffs the air, then steps back from the door as he smells the same scent I did.

"It's a trap," he mutters and I nod.

"Levver's Leaf, also known as Candy Floss Leaf. Poisonous when it comes into contact with the acid on our skin. If you'd touched that doorknob, you'd be dead in half an hour."

He clenches his fists. "Those fuckers. I hate traps."

"Don't we all. They must have known that we'd be able to detect the people in there. Do you have any gloves? I don't want to get this stuff on my clothes."

"No, didn't think of that when we rushed off. I'll get something from the kitchen."

While he runs downstairs, I extend my senses again, homing in on the two heartbeats on the other side of the door. I think they're getting even slower. Maybe they were given poison too, that would explain why they're not getting out of there. Accidental poisonings while putting Candy Floss Leaf on the doorknob, or innocent victims? We'll find out soon, I hope.

Ryker returns with a stack of tea towels, each more hideous than the next. Gill Delaney has terrible taste. I take one of them and carefully wrap it around my hand, making sure none of my skin is exposed. I don't have the antidote to Levver's Leaf with me and I doubt Ryker could make it home and back here in half an hour.

I exchange a look with him, then turn the doorknob. As soon as the door springs open, I let the dishcloth fall to the floor.

It's a small room, more of a cell than an actual room. A metal bed on either side, no windows, a flickering light bulb dangling from the ceiling.

I sway as images assault me, memories of my own cell that looked so very much like this one. The pain of their torture, the endless lonely nights, the hopelessness…

Ryker wraps an arm around my waist. He starts rubbing gentle circles on my lower back, anchoring me in the present. I don't meet his eyes. I don't want to see the pity in them.

I push away the memories and concentrate on what's happening right here, right now. To our right is a woman, unconscious, starved, shaved bald. She smells human. On the bed on the left is a man with sunken cheeks and a stubby beard. He must have been broad and muscular once, but just like the female prisoner, he's lost a lot of weight. How long have those two been here?

His heartbeat is stronger than the woman's. I shake his shoulders to see how deeply unconscious he is. He groans, but it's a guttural, uncontrolled sound. I gently lift his eyelids, checking his pupils. They're pinpricks, far smaller than they should be if this state is due to natural causes. I pull down his jaw, forcing his mouth to open slightly.

"Do you smell that?" Ryker asks. "Is that…apples?"

I nod. "Just what I thought. They've been poisoned too. Heltaskelter Juice, if I'm not mistaken. It sucks you dry like a vampire, increases your metabolism until your body starts devouring itself. These guys may look like they've been starved for weeks but it may have only been a few days."

The door downstairs opens just loud enough for me to hear. Either reinforcements or one of us.

"I'll go down and check," Ryker volunteers. "Unless you need me to help?"

I shake my head. "There's nothing we can do for them here. Bethany will be able to sort out an antidote, but nothing I have on me is any use. I'll come with you, it's not like they're going to walk away while we're gone."

Together, we race along the corridor and down the carpeted stairs. The blood from our footsteps has dried by now but I can still smell it. Maybe I'll get to fight this time. I breathe in deep and disappointment makes me groan.

It's Gryphon, not grunts to kill. The siren is standing next to the pile of bodies, looking at them appreciatively.

"I see you had fun."

"*He* had fun," I huff and nod towards Ryker. "I only got to kill one and that wasn't even as slow as I'd wanted."

Gryphon rolls his eyes, ignoring my complaints. "If you're done killing people, we have a bit of a situation at home. It might be best if you return with me immediately."

CHAPTER SIX

Two corpses await us in the hallway. They're propped up on chairs and my sisters are busy dressing them in garments that look like they've been taken from a grandmother's closet. Large hats, a pink dressing gown, fluffy slippers, a flowery dress with buttons on the front.

"What do you think?" Sophie asks brightly, wielding a pink umbrella that I've never seen before. She puts it in the hand of one of the corpses and grins. "Aren't they pretty?"

A girl her age shouldn't play with dead bodies. She should run away screaming or whatever else normal people do when confronted with death. I wonder if I should tell her that I killed her adoptive mother. I decide against it. She'll find out at some point, but I don't want to destroy this moment of fun for her.

"Sophie helped me decorate them," Caitlin says, stepping behind her little sister. "We're doing sisterly bonding."

I groan. That's been their excuse for every bit of mischief they've come up with. Apparently, sisterly bonding involves playing tricks on their other sister - me.

"Who are they and why did you dress them up?" I ask, suddenly feeling very old and grown-up. And tired.

"They tried to break in while you were gone," Gryphon explains from behind me. He's clearly trying hard not to laugh. "There were more than just these two. Girls, what did you do to them?"

"Nothing," Caitlin says, all innocence. "Bethany took them down into the morgue. She only left us these two so we could use them to give you a nice welcome."

I frown. "Is that what she said?"

"In as many words."

Was I this cheeky when I was her age? Probably. No, definitely. It's just weird to see it from the other side. I never dressed up a corpse in a pink gown and a sun hat though.

Lily appears at the end of the corridor, making the entrance hall feeling very crowded. "Hey, Kat. These guys were looking for you."

"Now they're no longer looking," Caitlin muttered under her breath.

Very clever. I don't deign her with a reaction and turn to Lily instead. "How many?"

"Six. They never got further than here. Some of Ryker's cats got involved; I owe them some extra catnip. They may be small, but they're excellent at distracting opponents in a fight."

"Catnip?" I ask before I can stop myself.

"Not for you. Remember what happened last week?"

I immediately grow sober. I had the worst flashbacks ever after taking a small dose of catnip. It was like I was back in my cell, being tortured by the floor heating up so much that my skin started to blister. Nowhere to run. All alone.

I shudder. I need to accept that I won't be able to take

any catnip for a while, not until my mind has settled and I've built barriers around those memories. At the moment, they're still too close to the surface. I've not had the time to lock them up along with all the crappy moments of my past.

"They came in as soon as you were gone," Lily continues. "They must have been watching the house."

"So they weren't looking for me?"

"I assume they were a message without even knowing it. Delaney sent them to their death, fully aware that they'd not survive breaking into the M.E.O.W. headquarters. Even if fewer of us had been home, we've got enough traps and defences to deal with only six intruders. He would have had to send a lot more to stand even the slightest chance."

She's right. "I guess he wants us to know that he's watching us. Well, so what. That's nothing new. And I left a message for him too. His dead wife."

"He won't be happy about that," Lily muses. "I guess we better strengthen our defences some more."

"I'm not so sure about that. He knew we were coming to the house. They'd set a trap, poison on door handles. Unless that was meant for someone else, Delaney may have left his wife there on purpose. Maybe he'd grown tired of her. Still, it's strange."

"Very strange," Gryphon confirms. "I'm going to call the mayor to help with the cleanup and to get those poisoned people either here or to a hospital."

"More poison?" Lily asks eagerly. "Looks like you had a whole lot of fun without me."

"We found two humans with Heltaskelter Juice in their system. Ryker stayed with them, just in case reinforcements arrive. He's got a couple of cats for backup, but we should probably get him some backup soon."

Gryphon pushes past the two corpses and disappears into the living room where we've got one of our two phones. The other's in the office; a room I've been avoiding because I can't be bothered with the paperwork waiting for me on my desk.

"How are the babies?" I ask Lily.

"Sleeping, last time I checked, but Tailie tried to strangle Furrie with his tail. It may have been an accident, but they're your kids so anything is possible."

"Is it bad if that makes me proud?"

Lily snorts. "Probably. I guess we should be glad Biter and Vamp haven't started suckling on their siblings."

"Is the naming ceremony still happening tonight?" Caitlin interrupts. "If not, I vote that you finally tell us the names you chose. The suspense is killing me."

Killing reminds me of the two corpses at my feet. "First you two need to clean up the mess you made. Bring those two in the morgue, then put the clothes in the washing. I have no idea whose bathrobe that is, but I doubt they want it smelling of grunt."

"It's mine," Lily gasps as if she's only realising now that one of the corpses is wearing her robe. "Did you break into my wardrobe?"

"It wasn't locked, so it's not breaking in," Sophie pipes up. I think we're being a bad influence on her.

Lily sighs. "Note to self, lock my wardrobe from now on. Heck, lock my room. I should have known leaving it unlocked was a bad idea with you little terrors around."

Both Sophie and Caitlin smile proudly at the compliment. Caitlin doesn't even complain at being called 'little'. At sixteen, she's at a stage where she refuses to be seen as a child, but also can't help join Sophie in her games. Despite her upbringing, she's more childlike than I ever was.

"I'll see if the babies are hungry," I announce. "Girls, clean up the hallway. Lily, make sure the house is secure just in case Delaney decides to do something stupid. And tell Bethany to prepare an antidote for Heltaskelter Juice. I doubt they have that at the local hospital."

"Kat!" Gryphon calls from the living room. "The mayor wants to talk to you!"

I sigh. Guess the babies will have to wait a little while longer before they can tear into my boobs.

*　*　*　*　*　*

LADY LARA HAS AN AMAZING PHONE VOICE. I COULD imagine her working at a call centre, easily charming people into buying useless products with a few simple words.

"Kat, I was going to call you today. Are you available for a chat? There's an issue I'd like your opinion on."

Typical, no greeting, no small talk. A woman after my own heart.

"I need to have a shower and change to make sure I don't have poison on my clothes, but then I could come over, yes."

"Lovely. Say in two hours?"

"Want to give me an inkling on what this is about?"

"Not over the phone, no. I'll let the receptionist know to expect you."

She hangs up without another word. I stare at the phone, curiosity warring with the desire to sit on the sofa and do nothing for a while.

Something wet touches my chest. I look down only to see a wet patch on my right boob. Great, I'm leaking again. With four babies to feed, my breasts are producing enough milk to rival a cow. I sometimes pump it into bottles to use while I'm not home, but once they've had their fill, there's rarely enough left for that. My babies are insatiable.

I head upstairs into the nursery. The three girls are sleeping, curled up around each other, but Tailie is awake, looking at me with his beautiful yellow eyes. He reminds me a bit of Ryker. Except for the tail. When shifted, Ryker's tail is thick and bushy, and when he's human... well, he's still thick.

I wish he was back already so that we can continue our moment from earlier. Maybe in the shower; we both need to clean up anyway.

Tailie reaches out to me and I pick him up, smiling when his tail immediately wraps around my arm. He's such a cute little thing. I can't believe I once saw them as parasites. Now, they're my babies, my flesh and blood. They'll never find out how they were conceived. I'll tell them that the guys are their fathers. Superfecundation will explain why they don't all look the same. For all I know, I may have the same reproductive ability as cats, being able to have my eggs fertilised by several different males.

"What shall I call you, little one?" I mutter and run my hand over his head. His black hair is growing nicely, the same colour as Furrie's fur. The twin girls have brown hair with a reddish tint, almost ginger. Their eyes are green, while Furrie's are a bright ocean blue. They were all born with the same blue eyes, but after the first two weeks, they started to change.

Tailie mews softly and I pull up my shirt, exposing my breast. Faint purple bruises tell of their last feeding. Thank the Great Kitty in the Sky that I heal fast. It still hurts, though, and I envy any human mother who doesn't have to contend with fangs.

He starts suckling greedily. His tiny hands hold on tight

and once again I'm glad that the babies weren't born with claws. I sit down in the armchair in the corner and get comfortable. This is going to take a while.

BY THE TIME I GET TO THE TOWN HALL, IT'S LATE afternoon. Ryker returned with the two poisoned humans just before I left, carried by some guys the mayor sent. Gryphon and Bethany are looking after them now, while Lily is playing babysitter. I sent Benjamin back to the manor to gather any intelligence he can find, hoping we might discover something new about the Fangs.

I never got the chance to have that shower with Ryker, but on the way out I told him in no uncertain terms that I expect him in my bed tonight. I still have my hammock for when I want to wallow in nostalgia, but most nights I sleep in a bed with one or more of the guys.

Lennox is still busy researching shifter babies. He's made a lot of new contacts in the past few weeks that may help us with other issues, too. His actual results have been meagre though, to say the least. Most of what he finds refers to wolf shifter pups and it seems they develop differently depending on how much wolf shifter DNA is still within their lineage. Wolves have fated mates and those are not always shifters themselves. Lennox told me that there are now some packs that have more humans and hybrids unable to shift than pure wolves. It's kind of stupid of evolution. One day, there may be no more wolf shifters left. Luckily, us cats can decide who we take as mates.

Lennox keeps saying that he's close to a breakthrough, but so far, that hasn't happened. Maybe we just have to accept that we won't know how the babies will develop until they get older and we see it first-hand. So far, they've not given us any cause to worry, bar the fact that Vamp and Biter could one day bite off my nipples. It's one of the reasons why Bethany is trying to synthesise my breast milk. For now, I have enough for the four of them, but they're growing fast and I doubt my body will be able to keep up with the milk production. I'm not a milk cow.

The receptionist gives me a wave and I step right into the elevator carrying me up to the top floor. A guard awaits me. I know he was vetted and trained by my guys. It was one of the things they did in exchange for Lady Lara's help in searching for me. In the end, I'd escaped myself without their help, but I appreciate the effort they put into it.

The guard gives me a sharp look but it's clear that he recognises me. He inclines his head and nods towards the mayor's office. I walk in without knocking, well aware that Lady Lara already knows I'm here. Nothing happens in the town hall without her knowing. After I was almost killed in this very office, she improved security.

I walk into her office without knocking. She's behind her desk as always, not in the slightest surprised that it's me, just as I predicted. Her frown turns into a smile and she gets up, pointing towards the two leather armchairs in a corner. It's her place for informal meetings and I keep wanting to steal one of those chairs for myself.

"Lovely to see you, Kat. Only an hour late, I think that's a record." She grins, clearly not offended at my lateness. She's used to it and I really needed that shower after feeding the babies.

"I've ordered us some tea and biscuits. Did I tell you I've got a new cook? She does the most amazing lemon butter biscuits, you'll love them."

I lick my lips in anticipation. I didn't have time to eat more than a quick sandwich and could do with something more substantial, but those biscuits do sound delicious.

We sit on the chairs - they're even comfier than I remembered - and look at each other in silence. We've only met twice since I returned to Attenburgh. The first time, I was still confined to bed and was slightly delirious. I have no idea what we talked about if we even had a proper conversation. The second time was a week ago when she came to our home to talk about her security detail with the guys. That used to be my job, but of course, the guys took over while I was gone. For now, I've not tried to take over again, but it did feel strange to have Lady Lara at our headquarters yet not visiting me. She did come into the office and we talked a little, but today is our first proper meeting.

She studies me as if she's looking for signs of illness or vulnerability. I do my best to look awake - even though I'm exhausted and would much rather be on my sofa at home - and look at her in return. Is that a grey hair tucked behind her right ear? Maybe it's a trick of the light. Her black hair is perfectly styled as always, shimmering just like her ebony skin. It must be some kind of cream she uses on her skin that makes her sparkle like a unicorn. Well, not quite as much, but I always love imagining that she's not quite human. She's too clever and powerful to be a simple human.

"See something you like?" she asks.

I'm tempted to reply with yes, but I'm not sure if that would constitute as flirting.

Instead, I ask, "Why am I here?"

Talking business is always a safer ground with her. When I'm around Lady Lara, I never quite know what to think. I admire her as a woman, as a politician, and I can't deny that she's stunning. Plus intelligent, sneaky and fearless. All attributes I'd want in a friend. Not that my friends have to be beautiful, but looking at some eye candy during our business meetings is rather nice.

"Let's wait until our tea arrives. I wouldn't want anyone to overhear what I'm about to tell you."

"You really know how to create suspense. I'll be disappointed if this is some boring politics stuff."

"No politics, I promise, at least not the kind you're thinking. In the end, everything is politics. Even when you do your *work*, that's politics."

"How so?"

"You decide who lives and dies. You can take or reject a contract, which means you make a choice that influences the lives of others."

"Making choices isn't politics. I don't care about the consequences. I just do this for the money."

She raises a perfectly manicured eyebrow. When does she even have time to go to a beauty salon? Or does she have her own stylist who visits her here? If so, I should better make sure they're vetted and not a security risk.

"I don't believe that. I thought we'd agreed not to lie to each other?"

I shrug. "It's not a lie if you believe it yourself. Or try to."

Lady Lara smiles warmly. "You're a better person than you think you are, Kat. But don't worry, I won't tell anyone, I know that would be bad for business."

A knock on the door interrupts our conversation. A maid sets a tray on the little table between our armchairs and disappears, closing the door behind her.

With a slowness that grinds against my patience, the mayor pours us some tea, then lays a biscuit on both our saucers. It's thin, elegant pottery that would break way too easily to be allowed in my household.

I almost rip the cup from her hand when she offers it to me.

"Tell me. Now."

She smirks, leans back and slowly sips her tea. This woman is trying to get killed.

"Maybe you should try meditation," she says innocently. "Mindfulness is supposed to help with controlling one's temper."

"I don't have a temper," I snap.

"Of course, you don't." She rolls her eyes in a very non-mayor like way, then puts her cup back on the table and rummages in her breast pocket. I try not to stare at her chest. Her breasts press against her azure blouse, perfectly shaped just like the rest of her.

What's wrong with me? Am I going into heat again? I shouldn't be ogling someone that isn't one of my three guys, least of all the mayor of Attenburgh.

She holds out her hand and I look away from her boobs at what she's showing me.

A very familiar bronze coin lies on her palm.

"Fuck."

CHAPTER SEVEN

I roll the coin back and forth, staring at the symbol carved into the metal. A square with a vertical dash cutting through it like a knife. I have no idea what the symbol means, but I know exactly who this coin belongs to.

The Fangs.

I tried to forget they exist. I've not had any problem with them since I moved to Attenburgh, or if I did, then I didn't know the people I dealt with were Fangs. I'd hoped I'd never have to get involved with them again.

"You recognise it," Lady Lara says quietly.

"I do. They poisoned shifter children back in my hometown. Well, not themselves, but they got others to do it for them. We found a coin like that when we raided a lab. They'd put poison in sweets that would only affect children with the shifter gene. We managed to distribute an antidote, but it was too late for some."

Mystery man's granddaughter, for example. Even though I now know he wasn't the benefactor he seemed, I still feel sorry for the girl's death. He may have deceived me my entire life, but that doesn't mean I can't have empathy for his relatives, especially a shifter like me.

"I remember, you told me once. It's awful, but not surprising. From the little I've learned about their organisation, they try to eliminate anyone that could threaten their power. Shifters can't be as easily influenced by their powers as humans, so you're seen as the biggest threat. Still, targeting children...that's abominable."

"Where did you get the coin?" I ask her.

"A murdered woman. The sixth that's been found dead in this part of town in the past month or so. Five women, two men. All of them had a Fang coin placed on their chests. I called Benjamin back when you were on your way back here, but I assume he didn't say anything?"

I shake my head. "I guess me arriving half-dead and with four new-born babies must have shocked him too much to remember."

"Yes, I can see why that would happen. I've tried to give you some time and have the police deal with it, but they're not getting any further. Besides, I can't tell them about the Fangs or sirens. I'm sure there are some sirens within the police force, but most of them are humans with no idea that anything supernatural even exists."

"So now you want me to find the murderer."

The mayor nods. "Obviously. The police haven't even been able to establish whether there's a connection between the victims or whether they were randomly targeted. The only common denominator is that they were all killed within half a mile of this building. I think it's a message to me. They wouldn't leave the Fang coins on the corpses otherwise."

"Have you had any strange letters? Phone calls? Anything that may be connected?"

"No. Nothing out of the ordinary. No one has been in

touch about this. If they're trying to tell me something, I don't know what."

I take a sip of tea, then dunk my lemon biscuit in it. Dunking biscuits is an art. You have to leave them in the hot liquid for just long enough for the biscuit to grow soft, but not too long or it will fall apart and you'll end up with sludge at the bottom of your cup. It's a matter of patience and experience. I think it should be part of every assassin's training. Dunking biscuits is almost like plunging a knife into someone's chest with the intention of keeping them alive. Having a knife stuck between your ribs is a great incentive to get you talking.

"Any idea what they might be doing?" Lady Lara asks. "Do you know if they've ever done something like that before?"

"No, the only time I ever engaged with them was the poisoning thing. My sisters may know more though. Ivy and Four knew about the Fangs when I first met them, but I never asked them why. It didn't seem important anymore after I left them so they could go to school and have a slightly normal life."

Lady Lara chuckles. "I wonder what you define as a normal life."

"One that doesn't involve being experimented on, killing others or having to depend on stealing for survival," I say immediately.

"You know that's kind of sad, right? Most people would have said something very different."

I shrug. "I'm not most people. But back to the killings. Are the bodies still around?"

"Yes, I had the police keep them in their morgue. Some of the relatives have been petitioning me to return them for burial, but I wanted to wait until you're well enough to take a look. I'll let the police chief know that someone will come to inspect the victims."

Me in a police station. That's never happened before.

"Make sure that nobody will be in the morgue with us. I may have to shift to find extra clues."

"Of course. But I will come with you. I want to see you work."

"Don't you have better things to do? Like ruling the city?"

Lady Lara tsks. "I don't rule. I just make sure everything works the way it's supposed to by giving others a little push in the right direction."

"Sure. And I'm a wonderful person who also gives people a push into a direction...towards death." I roll my eyes at her. "You're a ruler, there's no doubt about that. Authority is basically oozing from your pores. I'd understand your objections if I'd called you a dictator, but that's not what I said."

"This town has a council," she lectures me. "I'm just the public figurehead. I can't take all decisions by myself. As you said, it's not a dictatorship. But that's not what we were discussing. I'll join you in the police morgue. I'll also instruct one of my guards to show you the sites of the murders. Of course, the police have inspected everything there, but I assume you have other methods than them."

I can't resist a chuckle. "Indeed. Very different methods. Don't be surprised if you see more cats than usual running around the area in the coming days. They like to feel involved."

The mayor shrugs. "If one of them wants to join me in here for cuddles, she's very welcome. My grandma's cat used to lie on my feet in the winter; I remember how cosy that was."

I don't ask her if I can be said cat, even though the

thought of curling up around her gives me warm, fuzzy feelings in my stomach. I breathe in deep and suddenly notice something that's so far not registered in my mind.

"Do you have your period today?"

She gapes at me. "What?"

"Your period. You know, the devil's waterfall. Blood running from your vagina. Days of pain. Rings a bell?"

"Why on-" She sighs. "I don't even want to know why you're asking. Yes. Happy?"

That explains it. Why I suddenly feel so attracted to her. Must be her pheromones messing with my head. I smile in relief. I don't have to worry about my heart splitting into four rather than three pieces. It's just her body confusing my own. It'll be over the next time we meet. I hope.

"Did each murder victim have a Fang coin?" I ask quickly to change the topic.

"Yes. I didn't know at first; the police only told me about it after the third victim had the same coin on them. They didn't know what it was."

"Did you tell them?"

"No, obviously not. I don't need to involve the police in a siren-led criminal organisation aiming for world domination."

I laugh. "Some people would say that this is exactly what the police is for."

"Some people are idiots. This is better handled by agents outside the law, like you and M.E.O.W. Just make sure you'll leave one or two alive so the police can arrest them and feel like they've done something good."

I'm a little surprised to hear her talk like that, but I guess I still don't know everything about her and how she handles things. By now I should be aware that there's a lot more to her than meets the eye.

"Shall I meet you at the morgue tomorrow at 10?" she asks.

"Ten in the morning or evening."

Lady Lara chuckles. "I know your schedule is a little different from mine, but I try to be home by 10 pm. Anything else you need to know before we go there?"

"Do you have files for the victims?"

She nods and points towards her desk. "They're waiting there for you. Copies of the police files, so they should be pretty thorough. Again, as I said before, they weren't able to establish a link, but maybe you'll be able to spot something they missed. Keep me updated with whatever you find." She gets up, our meeting clearly at its end. "Tomorrow at ten?"

I sigh and snatch two more lemon biscuits from the table. "I guess so."

* * * * * *

Back home, Bethany is waiting for me. She barely lets me take off my boots before she assaults me with a barrage of words.

"I've given them the antidote and the guy has woken up. He's got lots to tell you but I already had him give me a summary. They were taken by some masked thugs a week ago and held hostage ever since. They're husband and wife and you won't believe who they are. It blows my mind still, especially that I didn't even hear that they're missing."

I hold up a hand. "Slow down. Who are they?"

She grins. "I think I should keep that to myself for now, increase the suspense."

I've got my knife at her throat before she can even blink. "I'm impatient today. Tell me."

Bethany takes a step back, away from my blade, and

shoots me an exasperated look. "Violence isn't the answer, Kat, you should know that by now. But alright then, they're the MacFays. *The* MacFays."

I don't get her excitement, mainly because I have no idea who they are.

"That rings a bell," I hedge. "Who are they again?"

"Oh my, you haven't got the faintest, do ya. You really need to get more involved in the town gossip, it's fascinating."

"Who are they?" I growl.

"Only two of the richest people in Attenburgh. They were at that Jewellers' Guild ball back before you were kidnapped. They do a lot of charity work and as far as I know, are allies of the mayor. Mrs MacFay is on the Council, while he's got a chain of restaurants. You'll find them at pretty much every single high society event and not just in Attenburgh. They're loaded, Kat. Think they'll reward us for saving them?"

"They should. What do you think your antidote is worth. A thousand darems?"

Bethany grins wolfishly. "At the very least. Plus we had to get them here. Transport costs are high at the moment."

"Definitely. Let's not mention that it was the mayor who paid for it."

"Yes, let's forget that. Do you want to see him now? I think he's got a lot more to share than he was willing to say to me."

"Because he didn't trust you or because he needs to be tortured?"

She shrugs. "Because I'm not the boss. You've got authority. I'm just a lowly servant."

Hah, I'm not going to let her forget that she said that. Lowly servant. She'll never live that one down.

I hang up my coat and put some of my weapons into

the makeshift armoury. I always keep at least two knives on me, especially now that our home has been breached, but I also want to be comfortable.

"I'll make some tea," Bethany offers. Wow, something's happened to her. She's never this nice unless there's something in it for her. Maybe she's only making tea for herself, not for me. That would make more sense.

Before I go downstairs into the part of the morgue that has recently been fashioned into a medical area – mostly for me but it comes in handy now – I check who else is home. Benjamin is in his room along with the fawn. I grin. I wonder what they're doing. I'd have thought that the deer would like to leave and be back in the wild, but it seems she's content being spoiled by Benjamin. I'll have to check in with him later to ask if he found anything of interest in the Delaney manor.

Cats are all over the house, mostly snoozing in nooks and crannies only cats can find. Ryker is upstairs with the litter, but there's no trace of Gryphon and Lennox. Lily is in the office, hopefully doing the paperwork I've been ignoring. My sisters aren't in, but I think I heard them talk about going shopping after they'd removed the two corpses from the hallway. As much as I hate going shopping, I kind of wish I could be with them for some sister time.

I stretch my back and roll my shoulders. The exercise earlier was good for my body, but it also showed how much out of shape I am. I should go for a run tonight, maybe take the guys with me and see if we can find a romantic moonlit lawn for some fun time. Although I think Ryker wants to talk. I sigh. I don't want to talk. I want them to get naked and fuck me so I can forget everything that's happened.

"Tea's ready!" Bethany calls from the kitchen. She's prepared a tray with three mugs for me to take downstairs.

I give her a quizzical look and she grins evilly. "Laced with some Mother's Milk. That should help get them talking. The green mug is safe."

I give it a sniff just to make sure. Mother's Milk, a potion that loosens the tongue and decreases inhibitions, is hard to detect, but my cat senses are sharp enough to spot the whiff of vanilla coming from the two blue mugs. It's not a truth potion per se, those don't exist, but it makes people more willing to talk. Bethany must have had trouble getting all the information she wanted from the MacFays if she's using Mother's Milk.

I grab the tray and put on my impassive, unreadable assassin mask. It's time to talk to our guests.

CHAPTER EIGHT

Mr MacFay glares at me when I enter the room. He's shaved and already looks a little less emaciated, although he clearly needs the wall's support to sit upright. A stack of used plates bears witness to all the food he and his wife must have eaten. It's one of the side effects of Heltaskelter Juice withdrawal. It makes you ravenous, so much so that victims have tried to eat their own flesh if they didn't have any food. Gryphon has given both an intravenous drip to help them back to full strength as soon as possible, but it will still take weeks for them to regain their previous weight. Mr MacFay will have to do a lot of workouts if he wants to get those muscles back; they're affected even more by the poison than fat deposits.

Mrs MacFay lifts her head but her eyes are glazed over. Someone's given her a woollen hat to cover her bald head, but it doesn't hide the sunken cheeks and skeletal limbs. It's going to be a long time until she can walk around in high society again.

"I'm Kat Feln," I introduce myself in my best business voice. "You're in my home."

"I demand you let us go immediately," MacFay barks, but his authority is undermined by him swaying when he tries to lean forward. He quickly sinks back against the wall, hiding his weakness.

I point at the door. "You can go whenever you like, but I doubt you'd make it far in your current state. We rescued you and will do our best to help you recover. You've already met Bethany, she's one of the best poison specialists out there. Gryphon, the doctor who assessed you when we first got you here, also has special expertise in everything to do with poisonings. You couldn't be in better hands. The mayor herself made sure you were brought here rather than the local hospital."

"The mayor?" he asks sceptically. "You know her?"

"I'm her special advisor," I explain, taking great pleasure in watching his expression turn to astonishment. "Before, I worked as her bodyguard and improved the security of both the town hall and her own home. As I said, you're in the best place possible."

He groans and all the bravado leaks out of him, leaving only a weak, tortured man. "I apologise, I misjudged you. Do you have anti-siren technology in this place?"

I try to hide my surprise but I'm not sure I'm successful. "You know about sirens?"

He scoffs. "It's how we ended up in the Delaney's captivity. I'd heard rumours about him and his involvement in a clandestine organisation, so we went to challenge him. I never expected him to assault us and keep us prisoner."

Pride is everyone's downfall. He must have thought that he and his wife were too important, too famous to be attacked.

I put the tray on a metal trolley between the two beds and take the green mug. I don't think they need the

Mother's Milk to talk, but it won't do them any harm. It might even help relax them a little.

"Dorothy, would you like some tea?" he asks his wife, warmth and concern swinging in his voice. He truly loves her, that's obvious from this simple interaction.

She nods and tries to sit up, but she's too weak. I help her, propping her up with some pillows, while mentally rolling my eyes at my kindness. I'm getting soft. I don't go as far as holding the mug to her lips though. If she can't drink on her own, her husband will have to help her. I'm not a nurse.

I let them sip some tea in silence, waiting for Mother's Milk to take effect. Dorothy's cheeks turn a pale pink, making her appear a little less like a ghost and more like a human being.

"How did you find out about sirens?" I ask after a couple of minutes.

Mr MacFay clears his throat, suddenly looking a little uncomfortable. "Have you ever come across Peter Tamari?"

I nod. "Scar beneath his eye, filthy rich, works for the Delaneys?"

"That's the one. He died a couple of months ago under mysterious circumstances. He owed me money, so I went to investigate whether I could get some of his daughter's inheritance. I don't remember much of that visit, which is what started it all."

"He came back completely dazed," Mrs MacFay says in a croaky, barely audible voice. "Like someone had messed with his head."

"She wanted to send me to a doctor," he nods towards his wife, "but I knew there was nothing wrong with me. I started reaching out to my network and got some very strange, very similar reports about Tamari. How he'd done business deals with people who later couldn't remember what they'd agreed to. How he'd risen in society from nothing without having any particular skills or even being particularly charming. It was suspicious, so I dug deeper and deeper until I came across some conspiracy theories. Supernatural beings living among us. Sirens, able to hex people with their voice."

"It sounded ridiculous at first, but when we heard the same thing again and again, it started to make sense," Dorothy adds. I wish she'd stop talking; it sounds like she's torturing herself with every word. But again, I'm not her carer.

"After we'd figured out what the Tamaris were, we made the connection to other families, including the Delaneys. They're all beautiful, wealthy, influential. Some have been powerful for generations, others come out of nowhere. It took months but we ended up with a shockingly long list of suspected sirens. Then one of the private investigators we'd hired turned up dead with a strange coin in his mouth where his tongue had been before."

I take out the Fang coin Lady Lara had given me. "A coin like this one?"

MacFay nods, staring at the bronze coin with hate. "That's how we came across the Fangs. How much do you know about them?"

"Enough to know how powerful they are, not enough to know who's part of them," I say, surprised by my honesty.

"That's right. We poured immense resources into the investigation but only resulted in a list of five suspected members. Lord Delaney was at the very top, so we went to confront him."

"That was very stupid, you're only human."

His eyes widen. "You say that as if you're not human."

"I'm not a siren, if that's what you're scared of."

Neither of them looks reassured by that.

"Are you…a werewolf?" Dorothy whispers.

I grin. "No, I'm not. But you should know that humans aren't alone in this world."

"Vampires?" she asks with wide eyes.

"No, they don't exist. Well, kind of, but let's focus on what's important."

I think back to how Gryphon told me that vampires were a kind of succubi who fed on all sorts of things, not just blood. I'd been heavily pregnant and had just bitten my siren. It must have been Vamp and Biter inside of me who somehow made me do that. Since then, I've not felt any urges to bite my mates.

"When you got us out of the Delaney mansion, did you capture the Delaneys?" Mr MacFay asks. "I can't seem to remember if I ever got the chance to challenge them and ask them the questions I'd planned to."

"Only Mrs Delaney was there. She's not a full siren though so you must have met her husband when you went to confront them. She wouldn't have been able to overpower the two of you."

"I didn't know that. Not that it matters, she wasn't involved in the Fangs."

I raise an eyebrow. "How do you know?"

"They're misogynist," Dorothy replies instead of her husband, sounding disapproving even with her broken voice. "They don't approve of women in positions of power."

"Hence the hate for the mayor," I mutter. "She knows about sirens, she's for democracy, she wants to help the poor, *and* she's a woman. She's everything they despise."

She nods. "And that's exactly why we support her. She's what Attenburgh has needed for a long time."

"Did you capture Lady Delaney?" her husband asks impatiently.

"Ehm, no. She's dead."

"But-"

"She tried to kill me," I interrupt coldly. "It was self-defence. Besides, they poisoned the two of you and would have watched you starve to death. You should have no pity for her."

"I don't, but she would have had information we need. It's going to be much harder to get it out of Lord Delaney. Now that his wife is dead, he'll likely go underground for a while."

"Don't worry, underground is where I work. I have people all over town looking for a trace of him."

When I say 'people', I obviously mean cats, but he doesn't have to know about my secret feline spy network. It's my biggest asset and the fewer people know about it, the better. Besides, that would start the whole 'I'm a shifter' conversation and I don't have time for that.

"Is there anything more about the Fangs that you can tell me?" I ask them.

Mr MacFay sighs deeply. "They're planning something big, that's all I know. I assume it's to do with the mayor since she's the biggest thorn in their side, but I don't have any proof. The whispers all sounded like it's going to happen soon."

The murders around the town hall must be the beginning of it. I'm going to ask Lady Lara to increase her personal security, although I assume she's already done so anyway. She's a smart cookie.

I get up and take their empty cups like the lovely, attentive woman I am. "Alright, I'll leave you to get some rest. If you can think of anything else, just tell one of the others and they'll fetch me. It's best if you stay here for a couple of days until we can be sure that the poison has been fully eradicated from your bloodstream."

"Could we have some books?" Dorothy whispers. "It's going to get boring."

"Of course. I'll ask Bethany to bring you some." I turn to Mr MacFay. "And I'll get you something to write. You're going to make me a list of all the Fang members and sirens you uncovered. Call it your payment for your stay here."

✺ ✺ ✺ ✺ ✺ ✺

BENJAMIN CORNERS ME WHEN I GET UPSTAIRS. "ARE WE still having the naming ceremony tonight?"

I want to say no – I have way too many other things to think about – but I should really put my litter first, right? The babies need better names than their current nicknames, Lily is right about that. I wanted to make this ceremony something special, but once again sirens have destroyed my plans. Yet another reason to make sure this town is and stays siren-free. With the exception of Gryphon and any other *good* sirens, of course.

"Alright, yes. Say in at sunset?" That should give me almost two hours to decide on names and deal with everything else.

"How romantic. I'll tell the others."

He turns to run off, but I grab his arm. "Did you find anything of interest in the Delaney manor?"

"A whole bag of Fang coins. They must have been distributing them. I also found a bundle of correspondence hidden underneath a floorboard."

"How very predictable."

"Yeah, I was disappointed by that. I've not had the

chance to read through those letters yet but I assume they're important if they were hidden away?"

"You can give them to me. I need to feed the babies and that'll give me something to do while they destroy my boobs."

A slight blush creeps over Benjamin's cheeks. None of the others has any problems with me nursing in front of them, but he's too close still to puberty to see it for the natural thing it is. Women have been nursing their babies ever since we crawled from the sea and turned into mammals, so men really shouldn't have an issue with it. They're lucky their nipples aren't being tortured by greedy mouths several times a day.

"I'll bring them upstairs," he promises. "And then I'll tell the others about the ceremony. Bethany has put a wager on the names you might choose."

"Has she now?" I laugh. "I better get my bet in quickly then."

"I'm not sure you're allowed to enter-" he begins but I shush him with another laugh.

"My house, my rules, my money. Now go get those letters. Oh, and bring our guests something to write. I'll be in the nursery feeding the babies."

His blush increases at the thought of going into that room while I've got my boobs out. He runs off quicker than ever.

Oh my, teasing my employees is way too much fun.

CHAPTER NINE

Tailie's got his tail around Biter's neck, but it seems more a friendly embrace than strangulation. Still, I gently pull them apart and press Tailie against my chest, encouraging him to feed. I always start with him or Furrie, leaving the fanged babies for last. It's slightly less painful that way, although Furrie has also developed a strong bite even without teeth.

My son wraps his tail around my upper arm and happily starts to suckle. I smile down at him, a warm fuzzy feeling threatening to burst from my chest. I don't know how to show the love I'm feeling for him, for all of them. It's too much to express, even if I was good at that sort of thing. Emotions have always confused me, especially when they're *my* emotions.

Benjamin arrives with a stack of letters held together with a thin cord just when Tailie is done with his dinner. He fell asleep as soon as I detached him from my breast and is now happily snoring away with the end of his tail in his mouth. I exchange him for Furrie, who's wide awake and is trying to tell me something with baby babble. She's going to be a big talker one day. Maybe she could become mayor like Lady Lara and rule the city with talk rather than weapons.

Benjamin runs from the room as soon as he's handed me the papers, red as a tomato and refreshingly speechless. I have to admit, I did flash my boob at him on purpose.

While Furrie drinks her fill, I open the first letter. It's addressed to Lord Delaney and is written in some sort of code. I could probably decipher that with some time, but right now I've got a greedy baby suckling on me and my brain isn't top of its game. The second letter is thankfully not in code. It's a thank you note to Delaney mentioning a donation. Money, I assume? It's signed by D.M. which doesn't tell me anything. I'll cross-check the initials with Mr MacFay's list later, maybe it's a match.

The third piece of paper is a list of addresses. In an ideal world, this would be the homes of all the Fang members, but I don't think I'm that lucky. There's no heading or any explanation what the addresses are, so there's no choice but to check them out one by one. Maybe I can put some cats on it. Ryker has taught some of his most trusted cats how to read a map, so he should be able to tell them where to go. It's not like they can read street signs and house numbers.

A meow interrupts me and I look up, surprised to see Pumpkin walk into the room. I've not seen him in a while; Ryker said he's busy ruling his own group of young cats. He's turned into a mini-Ryker, protecting fellow felines who require a safe home.

"Hey, little one. Come to visit the babies?"

He meows again and jumps on my lap. He gives Furrie a little lick – my daughter doesn't react, she's too busy drinking – and get comfortable. Typical.

"I'll have to get up in a moment to get the next baby," I warn him.

He gives me a look, a cat equivalent of a shrug, and closes his eyes. Looks like he's here to stay.

We still have no idea if he'll ever be able to shift. I really hope he will, but in the end, only time will tell. Ryker finally managed to shift in a life-or-death situation, and as much as I want Pumpkin to shift, I don't want him to get into one of those.

Pumpkin. Maybe I should name my children after vegetables, too. Carrot, Bean, Cabbage and Kale. That does have a nice ring to it.

I hear Gryphon and Lennox long before they enter the nursery.

My siren smiles at me with love almost sparking from his eyes, while Lennox bends down to press a kiss on my forehead.

"How are you?" he asks before kissing his daughter. She doesn't even look at her father, too busy sucking me dry. It's amazing how much these babies can drink.

"Tired," I admit. "It's been a long day."

"It has. Benjamin said you still want to go through with the ceremony."

I laugh. "Everyone else seems to want me to do it. I don't really have a choice."

Gryphon frowns. "Since when do you bow to the will of others?"

"You're right. It's not just because of that. I also want them to have proper names, even though it'll take a while to get used to it."

Lennox picks up Vamp from her cradle and gives her a tummy tickle. She squeals in delight and my heart fills with even more love. Can you die of an overflowing heart? I know it's possible to die from a broken heart, but this is the opposite. There's only so much a person should be able to feel.

"Has she grown from this morning?" my wolf asks.

"I wouldn't be surprised. It's not like these babies do what they're supposed to."

"I'm sorry I've not been able to find more on their development. I thought I was close to something but it turned out to be about wolves and I don't think it applies to our litter."

Our. I take in the way he holds Vamp, the way he looks at her. Gryphon has Biter in his arms, rocking her gently. They don't care that they're not the biological fathers. We're a family, no matter where the babies came from.

"You name them," I decide spontaneously, taking on Lily's suggestion from earlier. "One each. We all name one each. But we'll never tell them who named who; I wouldn't want them to feel like they're more loved by one of us than the others."

Gryphon's entire expression turns soft, like he's melting. Aww. "Are you sure?"

"I wouldn't have said it if I wasn't. We've talked about names and you all had suggestions. I don't want to make this decision on my own."

"But you didn't like any of the names…"

"I don't seem to like any name that isn't related to Catnip," I huff. "That's my fault, not yours. I'll name Tailie, you take one girl each."

Furrie uses that moment to bite my nipple. I gasp and pull her off my boob, inspecting the damage. She's broken through skin; a few small drops of blood are pooling to the surface. Furrie squeals in protest and struggles to get back to my nipple. I'm not sure if she wants more milk or the blood and I don't intend to find out. She's had enough, it's her sisters' turn.

Gryphon takes Furrie and hands me Biter. She's half-asleep, but smiles up at me and reaches out with one chubby arm. How adorable. I think I know now who my children's father is: The God of Cuteness. He must exist, right? My children are proof of it.

"Where is everyone?" Ryker shouts from downstairs. It's an act, really, of course, he can sense where we are. He joins us and leans against the door frame, taking in the scene. One big happy family. If only things could stay like they are now. Calm, safe, full of love. I never thought I'd one day crave such a simple life, but now that I've somehow acquired a massive family, things have changed.

But we're not safe yet. Not as long as Delaney and the Fangs are out there. Even if we get rid of Delaney, the Fangs and sirens present too much of a future risk. One day, they're going to decide to eliminate shifters. Or the competition, M.E.O.W. I'm no longer going to wait and be attacked. This time, we're going on the offensive.

"I was thinking," Ryker begins, clearing his throat. "I would really like to name one of the babies. I never had the chance with Pumpkin, his mother chose that name before she died. Unless-"

"We just decided the same thing," I tell him and his face lights up, his yellow eyes sparkling with joy. "You get to name one girl each while I find a name for Tailie. If we want to have the ceremony at sunset, you better hurry up. I'm going to take a shower once Biter and Vamp are done with their dinner."

Biter must have heard her name and bites deep into my breast. I yelp, but I'm used to it by now and don't let go of her. Yes, I almost did that the first time.

"Maybe we should keep calling you Biter," I groan and inspect the damage. Then look away. I didn't need to see that. Biter happily continues suckling, now mixing milk with blood. She's definitely my daughter, even though I've not craved blood since their birth. Even when I smelled all those dead grunts at the Delaney manor, I wasn't tempted to lick them.

"I'll join you," Gryphon says and points at my boobs. "As your physician, I have to make sure you don't faint from blood loss."

Ryker rolls his eyes. "It's my turn. Kat and I agreed that back when we were killing mutants. She promised me a shower together."

"Boys, the shower is big enough for three," I sigh. "Someone hand me Vamp, this little monster has had enough."

I give Biter a playful glare. She giggles and looks up at me with her big green eyes. I wipe her mouth with my sleeve, getting rid of the bloody evidence. Lennox takes her and Gryphon hands me little Vamp. I grit my teeth when she shows me her tiny but sharp fangs. This is going to hurt.

I'M SURROUNDED BY NAKED MEN AND I'M LOVING IT. WITH all three of them crowding me, the shower is a little small after all. Not that I'm complaining. I wouldn't want it any other way. Gryphon lowers himself to his knees, his hands wrap around my thighs and I let him push them apart, exposing my sex.

"Our pussy has a pretty pussy," he murmurs before teasing me with his tongue. His tongue is the best. Truly. I've never come across another man who's this skilled with just his tongue. I moan and lean back into Ryker's waiting arms. His chest is hard dend so is his erection pressing against my arse.

Lennox takes a soapy cloth and gently runs it over my breasts, leaving foamy traces over my skin. I like that he's at least pretending that we're having a shower to get clean.

Gryphon flicks his tongue and I forget about everything else. His fingers are on my thighs, holding me in place, steadying me, but he does more with his tongue than other men could ever do with their fingers. I close my eyes and cling to Ryker while Gryphon makes me descend into a crazed state of arousal. Lennox rubs my nipples between his fingers and I can't help but moan. These men will be my undoing.

I hiss in protest when Lennox's tongue suddenly disappears, but being picked up by Ryker and carried over to the bed makes up for it. He smells so familiar, like family, but not in the icky kind of way. He's mine, I'm his, and that's the end of it.

As soon as I'm on the bed, the duvet a soft, cool touch against my back, he spreads my legs.

"I'm sure there's a joke about the cat drinking the milk," Gryphon mutters with a wicked chuckle, but Ryker ignores him.

And then his tongue is there, lapping up my wetness, making my mind descend into fireworks. His tongue is rougher than that of Lennox. He doesn't so much stimulate me as eat me out. He cleans me with his tongue, preparing me for what's to come. That thought alone brings me right back to the edge.

Gryphon and Lennox lie down either side of me. Their bodies are warm against mine even though all of us are still wet from the shower, their touch a welcome reminder that we belong together. All my men are different, but when we're together like this, there is no difference between them at all. They're all equally mine. My love for them isn't finite, it's not split between them. It's for all three of them at once. It's hard to put into words what I feel for them, but I think they know.

Lennox cups my right breast and Gryphon massages the one on the left, as if they'd planned it. Ryker seems to have decided that I'm clean enough (let's not start mentioning milk again) and pushes a probing finger inside of me.

I'm so close to coming, but this time, I need to feel one of them in there.

"Fuck me," I demand.

"Stroke them," he shoots back, sounding more dominant than I'm used to.

I don't have to ask what he means. Lennox's and Gryphon's cocks are hard and erect.

I reach out and they both turn their hips a little towards me, making it easier for them to wrap my hands around their cocks.

Ryker seems satisfied and finally presses his cock against my entrance. I open my thighs a little further until he pushes in with one long, hard stroke. I can't help but moan at this feeling of completeness. Him inside me, touching the other two, their scents all over my body. This is how it's supposed to be. We're made for each other and we're going to prove that again and again.

Ryker sets the rhythm and I copy it, stroking the guys whenever he thrusts into me. He's starting slow, but once he's confident that I'm fully adjusted to his girth, he turns faster, wilder. Groans fill the air, interspersed with my moans as I teeter at the edge, so close to falling yet not able to take the final step.

"Touch me," I gasp to no one in particular and close my eyes. Fingers press against my nub, flicking it, and then I'm over the edge, the orgasm shaking me, making lightning flash before my eyes. Ryker pounds into me as my inner muscles squeeze him tight, while my hands are clenched around the guys' cocks, trying to keep up the rhythm while my body is quivering uncontrollably.

Ryker comes with a scream, ramming into me so hard that it hurts, but I don't care. The pain only adds to the ecstasy filling my brain.

Gryphon moves away from my touch, followed by the bed moving as he climbs down. As soon as Ryker pulls out of me, Gryphon takes his place, his cock continuing what Ryker started. The cat climbs into bed next to me and takes my hand, squeezing it tight as Gryphon fucks me hard.

Lennox breathes in sharply, then his fingers clamp around my wrist, pulling my hand away from his cock. "Give me a second," he pants, clearly trying to restrain himself.

Gryphon opens his mouth and a strange sound escapes him, one that makes me stop and then fall apart. I scream as an orgasm racks through me at the same time as Gryphon comes within me. We ride the waves together, holding each other until my breath slowly returns to normal. He wraps his arms around me and holds me tight, my breasts against his chest, my nipples hard on his skin.

"Oops," he whispers, but he doesn't sound sorry in the slightest.

My body is still shaking as bliss fills my cells. Siren-induced orgasms really are the best.

I let him hold me, stroke my hair, whisper soft words into my ear.

But we're not done yet. It's Lennox's turn and he lets me know by sliding off the bed, waiting for Gryphon to relinquish his place between my legs. The siren gently circles a finger around my folds, as if to say goodbye, then lets Lennox have his go.

He enters me in a hard stroke and I sense that he's barely holding on to the wild beast inside.

"Let go," I mutter, and he does.

He comes with a howl, pumping into me even as he roars his release. I cling to Ryker's hand while Gryphon snuggles against me, holding me tight.

We end up draped across the bed, all of them somehow managing to wrap themselves around me. Lennox cradles my head on his chest, his fingers playing with my hair. He's cleaned me up, making sure that I'm comfortable, before joining us on the bed. None of the human men I've been with ever did that. I am blessed to have found these guys, who not only care for me, but also for each other.

Ryker gently runs his hand up and down my belly, his touch light as the kiss of wind. His chest vibrates softly as if he's trying to purr. I smile, loving how he preserves his cat side even though he's human now.

Gryphon is on my other side, spooning my legs with his. His eyes are fixed on me, watching my every move.

"What?"

"I'm trying to figure out how I got here," he whispers. "One moment, I was a runaway hiding from my family, the next, I'm with a beautiful woman who's made me part of her own family. I'm not quite sure how it all happened. Or if I deserve it."

"Tell me about it. I was a cat all my life and now my human hands are touching this feline goddess."

"Stop it," I mutter. "You know I'm bad with compliments. Let's just enjoy a moment of silence before we have to return to the chaos."

And that's we do, snuggled together, our bodies connected, our hearts beating as one.

CHAPTER TEN

With all of us squeezed into the living room, the house feels a lot smaller than it is. I had hoped to do the ceremony outside, but it started raining and while I don't mind getting wet, I know the babies feel very different. They hate their baths, especially Biter, who puts up a fight every time we even get close to the bathroom.

We've put them into freshly washed clothes, but Furry has already managed to get some drool on her collar.

"Everyone ready?" Sophie asks, physically jumping up and down with excitement. Caitlin is almost as eager, although she's trying to hide it.

The guys and I are holding one baby each. As always, Tailie has his tail wrapped around my arm, hugging me back. It's the best feeling in the world. Closely behind is what the guys made me feel in the shower, though. We need to do that more often. Ryker wanted to talk more after, but I managed to stop him with ceremony preparations.

I never had a naming ceremony, or if I had, I can't

remember it. Same with Lennox and obviously Ryker didn't have one either, having grown up as a cat. Gryphon is the only one of us who both underwent an official naming as a baby and then witnessed it done for other children later on. He's been guiding us in what needs to be done.

Tailie increases his grip on me and I smile down at him. Like his sisters, he has no idea what's going on. He doesn't know what kind of life awaits him. He doesn't know the things his mother has done to survive. I look into his big golden eyes and hope with all my heart that he'll never have to go through any of the pain I experienced. He's going to have a wonderful childhood, I'll make sure of it. All four of my babies are going to grow up safe and happy, knowing that they're loved and cherished. I'll ensure they never know that they weren't planned, weren't wanted at first.

Gryphon clears his throat, looking extremely serious. "Please, everyone not holding a baby, sit down."

As soon as they're all seated, the room feels immediately less crowded. I breathe in deep, then focus on Gryphon as he looks at the babies one at a time.

"We welcome you to the world. Know you were loved from the moment we heard your tiny hearts beat for the very first time and that you will be loved until the day they beat no more. Our life together has only just begun, but from now on we will be part of your lives every second of the day. You are loved, you are cherished, you are treasured. May you know happiness, friendship and health. May you know right from wrong, your own true worth and peace throughout your lives. May you sing and laugh and play with only joy and never fear. Children, we welcome you to the world."

"We welcome you to the world," we all repeat

solemnly. I'm tempted to laugh at seeing everyone behaving so seriously, especially Bethany and Lily. In combination with Benjamin wearing a suit, it's kind of comical. Still, I resist the temptation by focusing my gaze on my children.

"Do you want to start, Kat?" he asks me quietly after a moment's silence.

I kind of wish he went first, but I get why he wants me to be the one to begin. I'm the mother, the woman who carried these four tiny people inside of me. Not for as long as mothers usually do, but I think the pain towards the end made up for that.

I take a deep breath and press Tailie closer against my chest. "I promise to make you the happiest children in the world," I say quietly, barely more than a whisper. "I will protect you with my life. I will steal you the stars and kill anyone wishing you harm. You will never want for anything. You will be raised with love and care. You will never lack for catnip."

"Kat!" Lily hisses. "That's not appropriate."

I flash my teeth at her and continue. "I name you Liat Feln. May your name serve you well." I gently kiss his forehead. Tailie – no, Liat – giggles and grins up at me. I don't think he understood any of it, but I'm glad he's not crying.

"Liat Feln," everyone echoes. I can almost hear Lily roll her eyes at my name choice, but she doesn't comment on it.

I step back and let Ryker take centre stage. He's cradling Biter who's fast asleep. Her brown hair seems to be growing with every day, much faster than that of her twin. We may have to give her a first haircut soon if this doesn't slow down.

"Little one," Ryker begins, lovingly smiling down at his

daughter. "We've been calling you Biter because you've been sinking your teeth into life from the moment you were born. You're a fighter, a warrior, and that's why I've chosen this name for you. Biter, I name you Bella after the belladonna plant. It may be one of the deadliest plants, but its flowers are as beautiful as its leaves are toxic. May you be as strong and deadly as the flower you're named after."

"Bella Feln," we all say solemnly before I meet his eyes and smile. He chose a good name.

To my surprise, Gryphon joins Ryker with little Vamp. Unlike her twin sister, she's wide awake and is taking in everything with rapt attention. "Let's make this short," he says while tickling his daughter under the chin. "You shall be Donna, the other part of belladonna. Together, you and Bella will be unstoppable."

My heart melts. Ryker and Gryphon must have agreed on this, which means they talked about names while I wasn't with them. They're behaving like true loving fathers. Which they are, I know that, but it's good to see yet more proof of it. My right eye itches. In other people, that might be a tear trying to squeeze through, but in my case, I'm sure it's just a speck of dust.

"Donna Feln," Gryphon says and we echo him.

Together, they step back and Lennox takes their place, holding Furrie.

"I'm not a poetic man," Lennox says with a shrug. "So I shall call you Shade. You may not blend in with humans, but once the sun sets, you will become one with the night. You'll move unseen unless you want to be noticed. You're something new, something beautiful, and I will make sure you'll never feel different within this family. And outside of this family, I'll kill anyone who hurts you with words or weapons." He grins down at her, a complete contrast to his words. "I love you, little Shade, just like I love your siblings. Welcome to the world."

Liat, Bella, Donna and Shade. I look at my babies and realise how well their names fit. The guys have done a great job. It won't be hard to let go of the nicknames and call them by their real names from now on.

Gryphon clears his throat again, getting everyone's attention. "The next part of the ceremony has been modified by Kat." He rolls his eyes with much drama before holding up a small bag. "Usually, we'd sprinkle flower petals over the babies, but Kat insisted that we use catnip instead. Help yourselves, just make sure they don't get any into their eyes."

Lily snorts. "Kat, you're incorrigible. Don't you dare pass on your addiction to my nieces."

"They're not your nieces."

"They sure are. If you tell them otherwise, I'll tell them of the time you played with a ball of string and almost licked your-"

"Alright," I interrupt her. Gryphon must not have heard that story yet for his eyes are wide open and he looks like he's about to combust with laughter. "They're your nieces. Now go cover them in catnip like you're supposed to. It's for good luck or something like that."

"It's a symbol of us promising to provide for them," Bethany corrects in a surprisingly sombre voice. "And I intend to keep that promise."

She takes the bag from Gryphon and pulls out a handful of dried catnip leaves. They're of the best quality, nice and big, not those tiny, shredded pieces you sometimes get with cat toys. Not that I've ever bought those.

Bethany gently lays a few leaves on each of the babies' foreheads, then hands the bag to Benjamin while shooting me a stern look. What happened to the fun-loving, never-serious Bethany? She's been spending a lot of time with the litter, maybe too much time.

One by one, my friends rub some catnip on the babies, until they smell so delicious that I want them all in my arms. Sadly, I'm not large enough – or maybe they're not small enough anymore. Instead, I breathe in deep, smelling the sweet aroma of my babies mixed with the addictive aroma of catnip.

I stand there with Liat on my arms, feeling a little out of sorts. Like this isn't quite real. I should be out there, running over the rooftops, assassinating people, doing what I was trained to do. Instead, I'm in a cosy, suburban living room with my family and friends, cooing over babies.

My life is unravelling and I'm not sure what to think of it. I both hate and love it. But once this ceremony is over, I need to get out of here for a moment and be Kat, the assassin again.

THE COOL, FRESH NIGHT AIR FILLS MY LUNGS AND I SUCK IT in, revelling in finally being outside again. I shifted as soon as I was a few blocks away from the house where the city dissolves into rural land and am now running as a cat. My paws barely make a sound as I fly over the fields, running as fast as I can. I rejoice in the way my muscles stretch and tense, propelling my large body forwards.

I'm free. A wild animal.

I run and run, not caring where I'm going. It's about the journey, not the destination. I only stop when my right front paw hits a sharp stone, painful enough to disturb my peaceful state of mind. I look at the damage, but it's barely bleeding. I lick the pink pads on my paw, giggling mentally at the tickling sensation. I'm not ticklish as a human but I am as a panther. Go figure that one out.

I'm at the edge of the Birchwood Forest, many miles away from Attenburgh. I've been here a few times before, but it's been a while, even considering my long Delaney-induced absence. I don't want to think of the sirens now, though. I simply want to enjoy this moment of peace, away from everything. Even from my family. I'm a cat; I'm a solitary creature. I'm trying hard to be social, but I realise now that I need to take time off more often. This is refilling my batteries – and I'm going to need a lot of energy in the coming weeks, I'm sure of it.

A strange scent hits my nostrils. I sniff the air, then snuffle, expelling the flies I just breathed in. Evil little demons. Nature has its downsides. I breathe in again to try and focus on that scent. It's familiar. Wolves, but not the good kind. It's a sickly sweet smell, reminding me of honey.

The memory rushes into my mind. Milk and honey. Their blood filling my mouth. The kitten I rescued. It was back home, shortly before we moved to Attenburgh. I was in a forest, just like I am now, and I came across three mutant wolves attacking a kitten. I killed them all – and then drank their blood. Saliva builds up in my mouth and I swallow, suddenly a little scared. I don't want to go feral again.

I breathe in again. Now I'm sure it's the same scent I smelled back then. Mutant wolves. Back then, Lennox had involved his employer, Mr Moon, who'd followed me back to the scene of the crime, so to speak. With the help of one of his Pride members, he'd figured out that a siren called the Hypnotisse had control over those wolves, but that was the last I'd heard of the matter. I assumed Mr Moon had dealt with it, but what if he hasn't? I don't want any feral wolves anywhere near my home. Only hours ago, I promised my babies that I'd keep them safe, and now siren-controlled wolves are in a forest nearby.

I flash my teeth towards the direction of the scent. Wolves, I'm coming for you.

CHAPTER ELEVEN

I find them in a clearing, all three of them snoring so loud that I'm amazed their lungs are still intact. Maybe it's a side effect of being mutants. Another side effect is that one of them has a human head and a wolf body. I can't help but shudder at the sight. I can do partial shifts when I want to, but he must be stuck like that. Not quite animal, not quite human. His hair seamlessly turns into fur at the back of his neck, but his shaggy beard is very distinct from the fur on his throat.

All three wolves stink of alcohol. A couple of villages lie on the outskirts of the forest, so they must have had a decent night of drinking at one of the pubs. I just hope they left the villagers alive.

The old Kat would have killed them in their sleep. I hesitate. If I kill them without giving them a chance to defend themselves, I'm no better than them. Besides, they may be mutants who escaped their creators. They may not be as big a threat as I fear. I need more information which means I need them awake.

The problem with that is that if I want to talk to them,

I need to be human, but I don't have any weapons on me. I can fight well without, but there are three of them, all of them equipped with sharp claws and teeth, and just one of me. Maybe I should kill two and keep the human-faced alive to question. That's better than killing all three, right?

I stretch my muscles, readying myself to strike when a new scent reaches me. Siren. And once again, it's familiar. Fuck. This isn't just any old siren. It's the Hypnotisse, the crazed siren Mr Moon was after. She's still alive. That changes things. These wolves must be under her control. At least that makes it easy. They're going to die before I go after her. Not because I owe Mr Moon anything, but because she's a threat to my family. Who knows, she might even work with the Attenburgh sirens if she's this close to the town. I remember Mr Moon telling me that she's part of a wealthy, powerful family, so who's to say that this family isn't based in Attenburgh.

Her scent is faint but still fresh. She can't have got far; she's only got two legs after all. I sneak further into the clearing, extend my claws and launch myself at the closest snoring werewolf.

My fur is drenched in blood, making it stick close to my skin. I need a bath, but I can't smell any river or lake nearby. No matter, I'm going to get more blood on me once I've killed the Hypnotisse. Luckily, I feel no urge to lick the mutant blood off my fur. That must have been a one-time thing, thank the Great Cat in the Sky. The fight has made me a little hungry though.

I follow the siren's scent away from the clearing and deeper into the woods. I expected her to be headed to a village or even Attenburgh, but it seems she's walking further away from civilisation. Strange. I wonder what she's up to. Maybe I should keep her alive until she's answered all my questions, but I remember that Mr Moon said that the Hypnotisse is strong enough to control shifters. I don't want to find out if that includes me. Curiosity killed the cat, etcetera.

She's stayed alive despite Mr Moon and his Pride – he didn't want to call his wolf followers his pack after leaving the Pack – hunting her, so she must be powerful indeed. I only met the werewolf once, but he struck me as both intelligent and capable.

The scent leads me to a faint path, barely more than a deer track. I stay to its side, unwilling to leave the thick brush that camouflages me even better than the darkness. There may be more mutant wolves out there and as much fun as it would be to fight them, I'm going to deal with the Hypnotisse first, preferably without interruptions.

I wish I had one of those siren disruptors with me. Lady Lara's scientists have turned her anti-siren technology into a portable device that's capable of weakening or even completely inhibiting siren powers. Gryphon told me that she tried it on him and while it didn't take away all of his powers, it was extremely uncomfortable and made it hard for him to influence even the most weak-minded. Lady Lara offered to have collars made with one of those little machines attached, but I'll be damned if I ever put on a collar again. Ryker considered it, but I think he refused because of me. I'd hate to see him – or any of my men and sisters – to wear a collar. The memory of having that metal thing around my neck, preventing me from shifting, keeping me under the Pack's control, is too painful.

I'll just have to be quick and surprise her before she can use her voice on me.

Her scent is getting stronger and by the time I see a flickering light in the distance, I can smell her perfume. If I knew anything about perfumes, I'd be able to identify it, but I've never used any. I wouldn't want to disguise my wild, feline scent. I doubt the guys would like that either.

A surprisingly large hut has been built in the centre of a clearing, much bigger than the one I killed the wolves in. The hut is old but in a good state; someone's maintained it or maybe it's even been lived in continuously. Who would want to live out here in the middle of nowhere though? Even I wouldn't want to. It's too far away from humans I'd want to kill. Too far away from decent food. I'd only live in a forest if I went feral and I don't intend on doing that ever again. My cat and I have merged, no longer separate, making us more powerful than we were before.

It must be the early hours of the morning by now, but there's still light in the hut. I extend my senses. Only one heartbeat; she's alone. I circle the hut, looking for any scents that might indicate that other people have been here, but I can only pick up the Hypnotisse and her wolves' scents.

The single-storey cabin has two doors, one to the front and a smaller one to the back. That one doesn't look like it's used a lot; moss is growing along the edges and a spider has woven a large, intricate web in a corner.

This door might squeak if I use it, so it's best to enter via the front or through a window. There are no attic windows, so my choice is limited. I listen out for the siren's heartbeat again. She's to my right, almost at the far wall of the house, and awake. Her breathing is regular and I doubt she knows I'm out here. That's good. I'll have the element of surprise. She doesn't know yet that her wolves are dead. They were quite a distance away from here so I assume her link to them doesn't extend this far.

I'm so tempted to interrogate her, but I have neither my weapons nor my poisons. Without knowing the extent of her powers, I won't take that risk. I may have in the past, but now I have others to think about. My babies will expect to drink from my boobs in the morning. I sigh. Now, as a panther, my nipples don't hurt, but I know that once I shift, they will be sore again. I heal fast, but not fast enough for my children's never-ending hunger.

The window it is. The one at the other end of the house is slightly open and gives me a better chance of getting in undetected than the front door. As soon as I reach the window, I shift in one fluid motion until I stand on only two legs. It aches a little, but I ignore the pain. I'm already looking forward to shifting back and running home on four paws again. I don't want this feline night-time adventure to be over yet.

Slowly and with as much patience as I can muster, I pull open the window. It creaks a little but not enough that a normal human would hear. I climb through, landing on the wooden floor in a crouch. The room contains only a single bed and a large wardrobe, both carved from birchwood. It almost smells like the forest in here. Rustic but pretty. The bed is covered in siren stink and I can't help but wrinkle my nose. For creatures so beautiful, their smell is diabolic, saying more about their true nature than their looks. The door leading to the rest of the house is closed, but I manage to open it without it screeching. The hut really is in good condition with well-oiled doors and spotless floors. Only the windows are dirty as if someone doesn't want others to be able to look inside.

A short hallway leads to two more rooms as well as the front entrance. It's dark in here, the only light coming from beneath the door at the other end of the corridor. I walk in the rhythm of her heartbeat until I can put my hand on the door handle. Now it's all about being fast. I need to run in and kill her in one movement. No hesitation. No questions.

I reach for my old assassin persona, putting it on like a cloak. No emotions. No qualms. Just the mark and me.

Life is surprisingly simple when you blend out everything but death. I hear her heartbeat as loud as if she were standing next to me. I smell her breath, her perfume. I sense her turning around just when I burst through the door. I take in the room, assessing it for threats, while at the same time running at the siren. A rustic, simple living room with an unlit fireplace. The candles on a low table throw flickering shadows across the Hypnotisse's face. Even in the dim light, she's stunning. Her blonde hair falls to her waist, reminding me of spun gold. She's got a robe wrapped around her slender body, but her feet are bare on the cold wooden floor. She opens her mouth, probably to sing me into submission, but I'm faster. My hands close around her throat and I topple her to the floor, landing on her, using her to cushion my fall.

She cries out in pain as her head crashes against a raised edge around the fireplace. Her eyes flicker close for a moment and I dare to hope that she's unconscious, but then they open again and she glares at me with pure hate. I better make this quick.

I squeeze my thumbs into her throat, shutting off her windpipe as well as her chance to use her magical vocal cords. She struggles under me, but she lacks the strength to get me off her. I evade her as she tries to scratch at my face and use my legs to keep her from buckling under me. I may be slightly smaller than her, but she doesn't look like she's ever had to do physical work in her life. Her muscles are non-existent, at least the ones on her body. Her facial muscles are a work of beauty as she makes the strangest grimaces. Maybe she thinks a pantomime performance will help her. Spoiler: it won't.

Her struggles slowly become less as I squeeze the life out of her. It's satisfying; I forgot how much I like strangulation. Recently, I've favoured my knives for everything, but maybe I should get myself a new garrotte. I listen to her heartbeat, ba-bum, ba-bum, which is getting slower after it had first shot up. Not much longer. She's at the edge of consciousness now, barely holding on. Her eyelids are drooping, but she's not stopped trying to defend herself. I have to give her that, she's persistent. And wants to stay alive, I guess, like all of us.

I breathe a sigh of relief when she finally falls unconscious. That took longer than it usually does, but maybe siren physiology is different. I keep my thumbs on her windpipe. A few minutes and she'll be dead. I have to decide now whether to kill her or dare keep her alive to question her. She's too heavy for me to drag her back to Attenburgh, but without anti-siren technology, I have no chance at interrogating her here. She'll try and get into my mind as soon as she's awake again. I need her to talk without singing me into submission, but that's impossible. Death it is.

I ignore the flicker of regret in the muddy depths of my conscience and squeeze off her airways until her heart stops beating. It's not regret for her death. It's because I won't get a chance to find out more about her plans.

A wolf howls in the distance and I sit up straight, extending my senses. It's definitely a shifter, but I can't tell whether it's one of the Hypnotisse's mutants or one of the good shifters. Well, *good* is relative.

Now that I'm listening more closely, I can hear several beings move through the brush, approaching this hut. Looks like I might get another fight. I leave the siren on the floor and search her house for weapons. I could shift to confront the wolves, but I still want to investigate this place and two shifts in a row will be exhausting.

She's got a nice assortment of butcher's knives in her kitchen; more than a one-person household should have. It suits me well. I take the two sharpest and take position behind the front door. If they enter the building that way, I'll be hidden from view for a few vital seconds.

The closer they get, the more information my senses can gather. Five wolves, all large and heavy. They make a lot of noise, disturbing the wildlife. Birds warn each other of the intruders, sounding tired and annoyed. My gaze flicks to a clock in the hallway. It's two in the morning. I should head back soon or I will miss the babies' breakfast. Which in turn means they'll be cranky all day; not something I want. One annoyed baby would be enough, but four of them…a nightmare.

When they enter the clearing, I finally get a whiff of their scent. Urgh. I won't get a fight. The tension seeps from me and I drop my knives as I walk outside to greet Mr Moon.

CHAPTER TWELVE

The Pride leader shifts as soon as I see him. Unlike me, he's naked. Shifter magic is weird and unpredictable. I wish he'd wear his usual leather coat though. He's in his mid-fifties and let's just say that he's no longer as fit in all parts of his bodies. His chest is toned, pure muscle, but below that…

I look up, focusing on his face instead. He's not changed at all. Grey streaks run through his curly black hair and an untamed beard covers most of his face. His eyes are like glimmering coals in the dark, full of power and the confidence of an alpha.

The four wolves behind him stay in their animal form. They're all black, blending well into the darkness. Mr Moon chose well in taking only them along and leaving the white and grey-furred wolves behind. Lennox always says how he wishes he could change his fur colour. His pure white coat is beautiful at day, especially paired with his sparkling blue eyes and the black spot on his forehead, but at night he's a liability. Easy to spot, easy to give everyone away.

"Miss Feln, I didn't expect to see you here," Mr Moon greets me in his deep, pleasant voice. This is what an aged whisky would sound like. "Am I right in thinking that we're too late?"

"If you intended to kill the Hypnotisse, then yes, you're too late. Sorry."

He sighs and suddenly looks a lot older. Maybe I was wrong when I estimated him to be in his fifties. It's always hard to tell with shifters; we live longer than humans, in theory, but that rarely happens because we usually die of unnatural circumstances long before we reach old age.

"I guess I should be glad she's gone, but I wish I'd been the one to do the deed. I hope you made her suffer?"

I open the door wider in an invitation for them to come in. "See for yourself. It was quicker than I would have wished, but I didn't want to give her the chance to enchant me."

"You confronted her without anti-siren tech?" he asks incredulously. "That was foolish."

"I never knew she was here," I defend myself. "I came across her by accident. I would have been a lot better prepared had I planned this."

"I don't believe in coincidences," he mutters as he walks past me into the hut. He heads straight to the living room, clearly guided by his wolf nose.

I join him and watch as he kneels by her side, examining her. "I had so many questions," he sighs, sounding a little annoyed. "Now it's too late."

One of his wolves joins us, a female. The light catches on something around her neck. I suck in a sharp breath when I realise it's a collar.

"Anti-siren," Mr Moon explains, following my gaze. "Ana has been kind enough to wear it, even though she was part of the Pack and has been forced to wear a collar in the past."

The wolf growls softly at the mention of the Pack and I empathise with her. I couldn't wear a collar again, not ever. I admire her for her strength of mind.

"I would have kept her alive if I'd had that at my disposal," I explain, "but as I said, I didn't even know she was in the area. If you'd got here a few minutes-"

I stare down at her lifeless body. She's still warm and except for her head wound, she's unharmed. Maybe a few bruises from the fall, but nothing that won't heal.

"I can't believe I'm suggesting this, but we could try and resuscitate her," I say slowly, feeling like I'm making a fool of myself with that proposal. I kill people, I don't bring them back to life.

"Isn't she braindead after strangulation?" he asks.

"Mhmm. You could be right. I'm good at killing people but I've never tried *unkilling* someone. On television, they'd do CPR."

Mr Moon smiles indulgently. I don't want to call it patronising because I don't want to start a fight with him. He turns to the door and shouts, "Jack!"

A black wolf with a grey patch on his chest prowls into the room and cocks his head at his alpha.

"We have need of your skills. Shift."

His transformation looks and sounds more painful than what I'm used to. By the time he's a fully-formed man, his forehead is covered in sweat and his eyes are lined with red. I've seen him before. He did some kind of magic where he used my memories to discover that the wolves had been with the Hypnotisse. Without his skills, we wouldn't have known who sent them. I'm not sure what he's going to do now, though. It's not like I ever let her speak, so there are no memories to look at.

"Yes, boss?" Jack asks. His grey-white goatee reminds me of the patch on his wolf-chest.

"You remember Kimdentown?"

Jack sighs. "Hard to forget. Please don't make me do that again."

"Please. Don't make me order you. We need the information and she's still warm. It shouldn't be too late."

"Wait, what are you talking about?" I interrupt.

Mr Moon turns to me. "Jack can't just see the echoes of the living. He can also look at the memories of the recently deceased."

"It's an imprecise science," Jack says, clearly not happy about it. "And it's extremely uncomfortable for me. When I enter the echo, I have to stay in it until the end. I have to experience the person's death. Was this one quick?"

I wish I could tell him it was, but I don't want to lie to the wolf and leave him unprepared. "Half a minute until she fell unconscious, then maybe two minutes until her heart stopped beating. She struggled quite a bit. Oh, and she hit her head when I toppled her."

Jack groans. "Great. Just what I needed."

"We can try and pull you out early," Mr Moon offers. It's clear to see that he cares about his Pride members, but he's also eager to get results. If Jack said no, I'm sure Mr Moon would order him to do it anyway. Lennox has told me about a wolf alpha's power over his pack. A strong alpha – and I'm sure Mr Moon is extremely strong – is able to force his wolves to do what he wants.

"No, I doubt that'll work. It might make things worse." Jack sighs again. "I better do this now before her echo fades. I'll try and dive as deep as I can, but I can't promise anything. This is only the second time I'm doing this on a corpse."

He sits by the Hypnotisse's side and crosses his legs, making himself comfortable. Laying a hand on her bloody forehead, he closes his eyes and relaxes. His entire body seems to lose all tension. I almost envy him. I've not been able to relax in…forever?

"Have you had a chance to look around yet?" Mr Moon asks me quietly, almost a whisper.

I shake my head. "You arrived before I could." I nod towards Jack. "Will this take long?"

"No idea. In Kimdentown, he was out for half an hour. I say we use the time to check if we can find out more about why the Hypnotisse was here. She's been travelling across the country using very strange routes that don't make sense. We lost track of her a few days ago until a local shifter contacted me to report a mysterious woman living on her own in the woods. We didn't even know it was her until we came across some dead mutant wolves. Your doing, I suppose?"

"Yeah, they got in my way. They're the reason I knew about the Hypnotisse; I'd never have searched for her otherwise. I didn't want her anywhere near my family though."

"Ah yes, Lennox told me. Congratulations."

I cringe. Are we about to descend into small talk about my babies? Better not. "Let's search this place. I'll take this room, you the bedroom?"

Mr Moon shrugs. "Alright. Holler if you find something."

THE SEARCH IS A TOTAL FLOP. ALL I FIND IS A PURSE containing a lot of money, a tiny mirror and a bright red lipstick. I give it a sniff, just in case it's laced with poison, but no such luck. This handbag could belong to anyone. I'm not sure what the purse of an evil siren should look like, but not as mundane as this. I do a quick sweep of the tiny kitchen but no luck there either. The knives I pocketed earlier were her most useful possessions. Unless she's got poison in her washing up liquid, there's nothing to be found here.

Before I can examine the bathroom - which is really only a wooden tub and a toilet over a hole in the ground since there's no running water in this cabin - Mr Moon returns from the bedroom, waving a single envelope.

"Hidden under one of the floorboards," he grins. "Just like in the books."

I didn't take him for much of a reader, but then, I don't know much about this man.

He holds out the envelope and I snatch it from his hand. A single sheet of paper is inside, slightly crinkled as if it got wet once and then dried again.

"Beloved daughter," I read, then look at Mr Moon with raised eyebrows. "What the fuck?"

"Read on," he encourages me with a smirk.

Beloved daughter,

I hope you're well. I have followed your progress from afar and am so very proud of you.

I'm afraid to tell you that our experiment has escaped and has taken my baby with her. Your father has followed them to Attenburgh and I'm preparing to join him there tomorrow by train. This unfortunate event may accelerate our plans, so this could be your chance to return to us. Your father doesn't know I'm writing to you, but I'm sure he'll reconsider your exile now that the nest is empty again, so to speak. Your skills will come in handy in the days to come and he will surely see that. He can be a stubborn man, but I believe I will be able to persuade him that your presence will bring more good than harm. Grass has grown over the events of the past and once we're finally in power, no one will care about what happened.

Please, join us in Attenburgh as soon as you can get there.

Your ever-loving mother

I want to puke by the time I've finished reading. *Our experiment.* That's me. This letter has been written by Gill Delaney, I have no doubt about it. Which means the Hypnotisse is the Delaneys' daughter.

"Did you know?" I ask Mr Moon.

"Know what?"

"That she's Lord Delaney's daughter."

"I'd heard rumours, but all I knew for sure is that she comes from a powerful siren family. It could have been any of the big ones. Why is that so important?"

He doesn't know. "Because Delaney kidnapped me and held me prisoner for months. Because he experimented on my sister. I killed his wife today. Now he's next on my list."

Mr Moon stares at me with wide eyes. "Lennox never told me who it was. I suppose he never had the opportunity to. Shortly after they found you, he called me to deal with a shifter issue, but that was all he said; he was clearly in a hurry. I've not spoken to him since. I simply assumed that he would have contacted me if you had…well, if you weren't alright."

I sigh. "I guess none of us ever suspected that the woman you were hunting was the daughter of my torturer. Not that it would have made a big difference. But now it does. Lord Delaney's daughter and wife are both dead.

He's not going to be happy. It might cause him to make mistakes."

He gives me a wolfish grin that makes the cat in me uncomfortable. "Let's hope so. We may have lost the Hypnotisse, but we will stand ready to assist if you need us. Her parents needed her for their plans, which means they likely involve wolves. She was the expert on controlling and experimenting on us."

"Moon!" Jack shouts from the living room and without hesitation, both of us run there.

The shifter is still on the floor next to the corpse, but while he looked very much alive before, he's now just as pale as her. He doesn't look strong enough to stand. Fuck. I had no idea this would affect him this much. I almost feel a little guilty. If I hadn't killed her, it would have been easier for Mr Moon and his Pride to get information from her.

"What did you see?" the alpha demands, but his eyes soften a little when he takes in Jack's appearance. "Do you want some water?"

Jack shakes his head. "I think it would come straight back up again. I just need a moment to rest before we move on."

"Of course."

"You might not say that once I've told you what I've seen." He visibly shudders. "Kat only killed a few of her mutants. There are many more, fifty at least, all of them converging on Attenburgh. She's been busy creating them. I've not seen many details but I think she spliced bear DNA and mixed it with ours. Some of the mutants barely look like wolves anymore and they're strong. We need to be careful."

"Fifty?" Mr Moon runs his fingers through his shaggy beard. "I'll alert the others. We need the whole Pride for this."

"I saw flashes of a call she had with her mother. Some posh woman. I didn't hear the whole conversation but enough to know what they're planning."

"What?" I ask sharply.

"They're planning to rule the entire country."

CHAPTER THIRTEEN

Lady Lara isn't happy about being woken at four in the morning, but as soon as she realises it's me, she opens the door and beckons me inside. This is her private apartment, one I've only ever been in once to assess the security. Ryker, Lennox and Gryphon follow me without a word. I've barely had a chance to tell them the basics after I returned to the house. It was more important to speak to the mayor.

She pulls her fluffy blue robe tighter around her body and beckons us to take a seat. Her living room is a lot more inviting than her office, but it still doesn't quite feel lived-in and like a home.

"When's the congress?" I ask without preamble.

She looks at me strangely. "How do you know about that?"

"When?"

"Two days from now. It's top-secret, how did you find out? I was only planning to tell you on the day so you could be my bodyguard. We've all been instructed to keep the information to ourselves. If someone asks, we're to say that it's a trade conference."

"What is it really?" Ryker asks, barely suppressing a yawn.

"A meeting of all the major towns' leaders and the government, including the Prime Minister. There's not been a gathering as big as this in, let's see, a decade at least. I've never even met the PM and now they're all coming to Attenburgh."

"Why here?" I question.

"It's not the capital or one of the biggest cities, so it's fairly inconspicuous. Low crime, not many media outlets who could report on it, enough good hotels for everyone to stay. Plus we've got a venue big enough for everyone. It was only decided two weeks ago that it would take place here. It's been a bit of a shock, to be honest. Usually, we're pretty much ignored by the government and left to do our own thing, as long as we pay our taxes, so this is unexpected."

"Do the people on the council know?" I ask.

"No. I'm the only one invited. If there are decisions taken that affect Attenburgh, I'll have to tell them that the congress took place, but they won't have any say in it." She rolls her eyes. "They won't be happy. They already think that I've got too much power. Not that I do have more than the previous mayors, but those were open to bribes and easier to manipulate. I'm my own woman."

She smiles proudly and I can't help but admire her. She's achieved a lot in a very short time.

"Why are you asking all this? You still haven't told me how you found out about it. If there's an information leak, I need to know."

"You remember how I told you about the collars they used at the Pack where Lennox and I grew up?"

"Yes, they stopped you from shifting and made you easier to control. Awful." She shivers and looks like she's about to reach out for my hand, but then leans back on the leather sofa and raises her eyebrows, encouraging me to continue.

"Not just easier to control. Some shifters lost their free will when wearing the collars. They became mindless slaves, following every command. Lennox and I were strong enough not to be fully under their control, but it did make it hard to rebel." I sigh and ready myself to tell her the news. This isn't going to be pretty. "A group of sirens, led by Lord Delaney, have developed a new kind of collar, except that it's not made for shifters. It's for humans."

Her eyes widen in shock. "Humans?"

"Yes, specifically you and all the other politicians gathering here. They're going to turn you into their puppets. A coup that doesn't involve toppling the people in power. To the people, it will look like everything's still the same. If politicians start coming up with laws suppressing them, they'll blame the politicians – you – without ever suspecting you may be controlled by others."

"That can't be true," Lady Lara stammers. "This isn't possible."

Gryphon clears his throat. "Trust me, it is. For a siren, shifters are harder to control than humans. I believe the previous collars worked only on shifters because most of them have an intrinsic urge to follow an alpha's commands. The collar replaced the alpha, exploiting that genetic vulnerability. Now they must have found a different way for collars to work, maybe copying siren abilities."

"You've started using anti-siren technology," I continue. "So have others. It would be only a matter of time until other politicians catch on and do the same. Lord Delaney is the Prime Minister's advisor. I doubt he got there with simply using his charming personality. We can assume that the PM is being controlled by sirens already and has been for a while. The development of anti-siren tech now forced them to take this step, making sure you're all able to be controlled."

"How do you know?" the mayor whispers.

"The Delaney's have a daughter. She's dead now, just like her mother, but we were able to get some information from her." I don't mention that the Hypnotisse was already dead by the time we syphoned the intelligence from her. "She was on the way here to help with the siren plan. We're not a hundred per cent sure what her role was going to be, but she was in control of mutant wolf shifters, far stronger than your average shifter. Maybe they wanted her to provide the security for the event, making sure nobody escaped while the collars were put on you and the other politicians. I assume all of you were planning to bring bodyguards, so having her and her mutants would have made it easy to deal with those."

"Most sirens don't have fighting skills," Gryphon explains. "They're used to manipulating those around them with their minds. They need others to do the dirty work for them."

"But…" Lady Lara stammers. I've never seen her lose her composure like this. It's like her confidence has drained away within seconds. "How can they do that?"

"Humans are at the bottom of the food chain," I tell her, sounding harsher than I intended. "You don't know it, but it's true. Sirens and shifters have evolved further. To be honest, it's a surprise the sirens have stayed in the background this long. I suppose it makes it easier if you don't have to do all the paperwork yourself. All this time, they've filled their coffers, lived at the expense of others, while making sure their interests were always protected.

You can be sure that Delaney isn't the only siren who's got a role high up in politics."

Gryphon pulls a note from his pocket. "The MacFays have given us this list of important people who they think are sirens. I've not had a chance to confirm it yet, but Ryker's cats are on it."

Ryker nods. "I've trained some of them to sniff out the difference between humans and sirens. No guarantee that my cats will find the people on the list though, it's not like they can ask them their name to make sure."

"Which is why I shall investigate tomorrow," Gryphon adds. "First thing. But now we should get home, Kat hasn't slept at all."

I get up and realise how heavy my boobs have become. I groan. "And I need to feed the litter. Now I know why people in the past had wet nurses."

BY THE TIME WE GET HOME, THE SUN IS SLOWLY RISING over the horizon, drenching the world in orange light. I roll my shoulder and turn towards the sun, letting it caress my face. I wish I could curl up out here and sleep for at least a day. Instead, I have babies to feed and plans to make.

At least the guys had some sleep. I've been up for what feels like forever. I've broken into a guarded manor house, killed an important woman, freed two captives and interrogated them, had a naming ceremony, killed some mutant wolves and their leader, and then on top of that woke the mayor for a crisis meeting. I should get a medal for squeezing all that into one day. It's no surprise I'm shattered.

I almost fall asleep while feeding the babies, although their nips and bites stop me from fully slipping into the land of dreams. Ryker is by my side, taking one baby and handing me the next, making sure I don't have to get up from my nursing chair. When he passes me Vamp - no, Donna - he stifles a yawn. He may have had a few hours shut-eye while I was out running, but it wasn't enough.

Donna latches on and clutches my boob with her tiny hands. She does a little chirpy sound while drinking, almost a purr. I exchange a look with Ryker and he grins happily.

"Yes, that was a purr. Her first proper purr. I'm so glad I stayed awake with you."

I stroke Donna's head and smile down at her. Her eyes are closed, hiding her bright green pupils. She looks so cute that I want to bite her.

Once she's finally done, I stagger to the bedroom where Gryphon and Lennox are already spread out, deep asleep. How dare they. Gryphon's arm is spread out so his hand touches Lennox's shoulder, which means they take up the entire bed. I sigh. I'm too tired to fight for space on my own bed.

"Next door?" Ryker whispers and I nod, grateful he understands without me telling him.

We snuggle up on the smaller bed in the guest room, him spooning me from behind. I'm too tired to protest and simply let his embrace carry me into the depths of sleep.

THE SMELL OF BACON WAKES ME. I LICK MY LIPS AND OPEN up wide. A rash of crispy bacon is lowered into my mouth and I rip it out of Lennox's hand with my eyes still closed. It's perfect.

"Did you put some catnip syrup on it?" I ask after devouring the bacon in record speed.

"Don't tell Lily. She doesn't approve."

I groan. "She never approves of anything fun. I think she didn't just hide my catnip supply, she threw it away."

"No, she didn't. I know where it is."

I open my eyes and glare at him. "You do?"

"Not telling you. I'll keep it for special occasions." I throw my pillow at him, but he evades it easily. "Call it my insurance policy."

"Why would you need insurance?" I ask before snatching the second piece of bacon from his hand.

"You won't leave me while I have the catnip."

I stop chewing and simply stare at him. He's not meeting my eyes, but his heartbeat gets faster. I sit up straight and reach out to him, pulling him close until he ends up sitting on the bed next to me.

"I have no intentions of leaving you," I say firmly. "You're stuck with me. But why would you even think that?"

"It doesn't matter. Shall we have proper breakfast?"

He motions to get up but I'm faster. I grab his chin and force him to look at me. "Tell me."

"I shouldn't have said that. It's fine."

"Do I need to get my knives?"

Lennox grimaces, then looks down at the bed, making sure not to look me in the eyes. A cold fear is slowly running down my back. Does he want to break up with me? Did I do something wrong?

"When you were gone, kidnapped I mean, I missed you. At first, I didn't know how to go on. Life without you seemed pointless. I know that sounds stupid because it's not like we've been together for years, but that's what it felt like. Everything was so empty. Yes, the others were still there and we kept ourselves busy with searching for you, but it was the worst time of my life. And that includes being collared and enslaved by the Pack."

I take his hands and squeeze them, putting as much love into that touch as I can. I want to hug him, but I know there's more he wants to say.

"When we found you, it was like the sun had finally risen after months of darkness. You weren't in the best condition, but you were alive and back with us. I thought life could go back to normal..."

"But then I had four babies," I complete his sentence with a smile that feels fake.

"That's not what I was going to say. The babies were unexpected, yes, but that's not the problem. My heart broke when you were taken. It's the same for the others; we've talked about it. We were shattered into pieces and you were the only one able to put them back together. Make us whole again. But..."

This time, I wait out the silence and don't interrupt. It hurts to hear this. It's more painful than any physical pain he could inflict on me.

"But you didn't feel the same," he blurts out. "Did you miss us as much as we missed you? Were you as broken? Or could you have gone on without us, living your solitary life once again?"

His questions hit me like blades, stabbing deep into my heart.

"Broken?" I ask quietly. "Of course I was broken. Of course I missed you. The thought of you out there was the only thing that kept me sane. Without you, I would have given in to Delaney's torture. So yes, I missed you. I was broken. I still am. I'm sorry if you don't see that, but it's the truth. I'm not good at showing what I feel. You know that, you've known me all my life. What am I supposed to do? Sit and cry? I can't do that. I've got children to look after now. I've got responsibilities."

The pain has given way to anger, red hot and searing.

How dare he. I was the one abducted, tortured, experimented on, not him. He only had to cope with my absence. So he missed me. Good. I'd expect that from my partner. Why does he think I didn't miss him? That I'd leave him? I just don't get it.

"I know," he mutters. "I know, trust me. But-"

"No buts. You can't expect me to lie here and mope about how much I missed you. What do I need to do to convince you? Cry? Grovel?"

He sighs deeply. "Talk to us. That's all we ask. What I ask. Don't keep it all locked away. I know you love me, my heart knows that, but I need to hear it occasionally too. You're not an emotional person, I get that. Just...I love you. And I need more. More of you."

"Maybe you should have realised that before you agreed to share me," I snap. "You can only have a third of me."

"That's not what I mean and you know it. I'm fine with our family being a little bigger than the usual. I've got used to having Ryker and Gryphon around. You deserve them to be part of your life. But I can't help but feel like you're pushing us away and it hurts."

Just like his words hurt. Every single one is a painful stab into the centre of my heart. My anger slowly drains away, leaving nothing but emptiness and exhaustion.

"I don't know what to do," I mutter, horrified that I'm actually saying this. I shouldn't. This is private. But then, this is exactly what he's talking about. I need to share more. Even if it's fucking embarrassing. "I don't know how to show you what I feel. How do I know what's enough, how much you need?"

"I'm not sure. This is all new to me too. I've never been in a relationship before this, either. But I think we need to talk. You need to tell us what happened to you. No more secrets. Let's put everything out in the open. We've already told you a lot about what we were up to while you were captured, but I'm happy to answer whatever questions you may have. I think we mostly talked about what we did, not what we felt."

"Well, you just told me that you missed me. That's enough for me."

But I have to admit, it did feel nice to hear him say it. That he loves me. Maybe he's right, maybe we need to tell each other that more often. I assumed that they'd know, but it seems my men are idiots and don't see what's right in front of them. Typical.

"Yes, we'll talk," I concede. "But not now. We've got a siren attack coming, plus I still haven't had the time to look into the murders near the town hall. And I need to talk to the MacFays again. And-"

"No," he interrupts me brusquely. "If you're serious about working on us, you'll have to put us first. I know these things are important, but so are we. There'll always be something else that gets in the way. Yet another murder, another case. Stop putting us second. We're your family and we deserve to be a priority."

"I feed the babies all the-"

"Stop." He gets up and stares me down. He's angry, but there's more shimmering in those beautiful eyes of his. Disappointment? I hope not. I don't want to let him down. He's my oldest friend and as much as I hate to admit it, I care what he thinks. I don't want to be without him.

Oh my, I'm about to puke. Too much emotion. How often have I mentally used the L-word now? I'm overdosing on love. That's dangerous for an assassin like me.

"We're going to talk now," he commands.

To my surprise, I nod. My body seemed to agree with him before my mind could catch up. Is this really the time?

I don't think so. I've got things to do - but he's right, there'll always be *things*.

"Alright. Are the others around?"

I already know they are, I sensed them when I woke up. It's something I no longer have to consciously think about. I automatically search out for my mates, making sure I always know where they are. Maybe that's something I should tell them too. It might make them feel all warm and fuzzy.

"You don't have to answer that," I say quickly before he has a chance to reply. "I already know. I always know."

He gives me a small smile. "Let's have breakfast first. It's no good doing this on an empty stomach. After all, you ate all my bacon. I'm starving."

I grin, a little unsure of what's about to happen but I know there's no other way.

I'll have to battle my way through this like I always do.

CHAPTER FOURTEEN

F orget being tortured. This is worse.

The three guys are sitting opposite me and I feel like I'm on trial for my crimes. They're squeezed together on a sofa too small for that and it looks as uncomfortable as I feel. I shouldn't have agreed to this.

I crack my knuckles, breaking the silence. How I wish I could hit something right now. Or someone. Preferably involving a lot of blood and death.

Lily has agreed to babysit while we're doing our 'intervention'. That's what she called it while giggling evilly. She knows exactly how much I hate this. Talking about my feelings. Bah. What a waste of time.

"We've gathered here today-" Gryphon starts and I start laughing. I can't help it.

"Seriously?"

He shrugs. "I wanted to make it sound grown-up."

"You made it sound like a wedding or maybe a funeral. Please don't tell me we're marrying?"

Their faces are priceless. In a scary sort of way. Ouch. Did they actually plan to propose? I surely hope not. For one, we'd never find anyone willing to marry all four of us. Attenburgh is pretty advanced in their ways but not that much. And besides, I've never had any intentions of getting married. I was collared to the Pack all my childhood; I don't need a new leash tying me to someone.

"We're not," he says tonelessly. "I suppose we should start by telling you why we wanted to do this."

"You don't have to. Ryker and Lennox already did that. Extensively."

Ryker has the decency to blush a little, but Lennox simply smiles at me smugly. He's happy he got his way. Prepare for my revenge, pup, it'll be sweet and taste of catnip.

"But I haven't. Before you begin, I just want to tell you that I love you. I've said that before and I will say it again and again, as often as it needs saying."

"I love you too," I mutter under my breath.

He chuckles. "I love to hear you say that. It feels right, like the truest statement ever spoken."

"Stop being such a poet." Lennox elbows him in the ribs. "Do your knife metaphor."

"Knife metaphor?" I ask curiously.

Gryphon sighs. "I was saving that one for later. But alright then. Imagine a blade, sharp and of the best quality. It's the kind of dagger every assassin dreams of. There's only one problem: it's covered in the dried blood of its previous victims. So much blood that it's started to rust. Now it's no longer sharp, no longer reliable. If we want to make the knife as good as new again, we'll have to wipe off the blood and polish it. And-"

"So I'm the knife?" I interrupt. "Are you calling me rusty?"

Ryker snorts. "I told you that metaphor was silly, but you two idiots didn't listen."

"Not silly," Gryphon grumbles, giving me puppy eyes. Shouldn't that be Lennox's job?

"If you want to clean me, we could take this to the shower," I suggest. "I'm up for it."

Lennox wiggles his finger at me. "Stop trying to distract us. It's not working."

I flutter my eyelashes and push out my boobs. "It's not?"

Gryphon laughs. "Kat, you're a lot of things, but a seductress is not one of them."

I shoot him a deadly stare. "Just wait until I've got you tied down on the bed and-"

"Kat," Ryker interrupts. "Back to the issue at hand or we'll be here all day. As much as I love spending time with you, we're all aware of what's happening out there. So, are you ready to share?"

I shake my head. "Not really."

His eyes soften. "What can we do to make it easier? How can I help?"

"Can't we leave the past in the past? It's no use digging up dead horses. The present is far more important than what happened."

"Not if the past influences the present," Gryphon argues. "It's affecting us, our relationship. I'm sure you can see that."

"Yes," I admit grudgingly.

"Then let's do this. We never found out what happened to you. Is it good for you to bury it all inside of you? I doubt it."

"You know he kept me prisoner," I hedge. "You know I met Sophie there and escaped with her. And you know that he somehow made me pregnant without me knowing. He said he experimented on me, but I can't remember. Either

I was unconscious or he messed with my memory. Either way, you know all there is to know."

Ryker gets up and swaps sofa, sitting next to me. He takes my hands and squeezes them gently. "We know that, yes, but what did you feel? How did you survive without going crazy?"

I look at him, focusing on his large yellow eyes. The cat in me purrs and wants to lick him. Not the time, pussy cat.

"Obviously I missed you," I begin slowly. "I worried about you. I didn't know if you were alright. My captor knew where I lived, so there was always the possibility that he'd returned and harmed you all. And... I was scared."

I sigh. It's hard to admit that. But it's true. I was scared shitless.

"At first, it was easy to resist. I thought I'd get out of there soon. This wasn't my first time stuck in a cell and until then, I'd always escaped. But then they started torturing me..." My voice breaks off and I use the moment of silence to gather my thoughts. How much do I want to tell them? I don't want to divulge too much. I don't want them to see me as weak.

"Go on," Ryker encourages me with a warm, patient smile. "We won't think any less of you, no matter what you did to survive. You're not weak, you're the strongest woman any of us have ever met. We're here with you."

I sigh deeply once more. This is the crossroads. I can either continue my silence and just get on with life, or I can drag out the past for them all to see. They'll see *me*. My fears, my failures. Am I ready for that?

Ryker squeezes my hand again and suddenly I realise that yes, I am ready.

"I was terrified," I begin and then the words come tumbling from my mouth. They soak them up, listening intently. And with every word, I feel a little lighter.

❋ ❋ ❋ ❋

Finally, we're on our way to the town hall, all four of us. Sophie had made us some lunch, which I needed after all that emotional exhaustion. It was surprisingly good to talk about it though. Not that I'm going to make a habit of it. In the end, they all hugged me and I almost cried. Almost. I'm not that far gone yet. But I was very close, admittedly. My eyes still sting a little when I think of how they told me how proud they were, how much they loved me. I'm still not quite sure why they needed this so much, but I'm glad it's done. In Gryphon's words, the rust has been rubbed off the blade and now it can sting again.

And that's exactly what we're about to do. First, we're going to talk to Lady Lara again. Then we're going after the sirens. We won't even give them the opportunity to go after the politicians. We'll strike them now before they can act. Thanks to the MacFays, we now have a list of four targets. We'll strike them at the same time. Not to kill, not quite yet. First, we're going to force them to tell us everything. All their other siren contacts. Then we'll go after them. And the next. And so on until all of Attenburgh has been cleansed.

Benjamin has equipped each of us with an anti-siren device - except for Gryphon, obviously. That should help us immensely. Gryphon said that he doesn't expect any of them to be as strong as the Hypnotisse, but who knows. Better safe than sorry.

We have no idea of these four people are strong sirens or not. They could be the bottom feeders of the Fangs, but we won't know until we kill them. We're heading to the town hall first to let Lady Lara take a look at the list. Maybe she'll recognise the names and can tell us something about our targets. We could have done some research ourselves, but there's no time. We have to act quickly and the guys' little intervention took up too much time already.

The receptionist looks at us with a bored expression. "Do you have an appointment?"

"No, but Lady Lara will want to see us," I reply. I know that man, he's let me in dozens of times before, but he keeps having a stick in his arse. What a bore.

"I'll give her a call," he says with a dubious look as if he can't believe that the mayor would want to talk to us.

"No need," I hiss impatiently and head right to the elevator.

"Don't we need his permission to use operate the elevator?" Lennox asks. "I've never been able to walk in just like that."

I flash him a grin. "Organising the security of this place has its advantages."

I press the buttons for the third and fifth floor at the same time and hold them down until a dong chimes and the elevator starts moving upwards. "Override," I explain cheerily. "Don't tell anyone. I'm not supposed to use it unless it's an emergency, but dealing with that receptionist counts as one, right?"

The guys nod, although I'm sure they just do it to placate me. They're well aware of how much I've sacrificed for them today, so hopefully, they'll treat me like a queen for the next few days.

Lady Lara is waiting for us as soon as we step out of the elevator. Mr Grumpy Receptionist must have alerted her.

"I thought you'd be here earlier," she says instead of a greeting. "What took you so long?"

I roll my eyes. "Personal stuff. And we won't stay long.

Just a few questions before we start the fun part of our work."

"Don't tell me. Plausible deniability." She leads us into her office and sits behind her desk, her fingers pursed beneath her chin. "So?"

I hand her the list of names. "Four people who're very likely to be Fangs or at least sirens. Delaney is one of them, but I'll deal with him after. First I want to get rid of his supporters. Do you recognise any of these?"

"Daniel Mason," she mutters, reading the first name. The initials are the same as in that letter Benjamin found, but of course, I can't be sure it's the same person. There must be hundreds of D.M.s in Attenburgh.

"That's a councillor. Fairly young, it's always amazed me how he managed to rise to his position this quickly. Very conservative views, especially for someone so young. When I first met him, I thought he might be on my side, but the opposite was true." She runs her eyes over the other names but shakes her head. "The others don't mean anything to me. The last one sounds slightly familiar, but I meet a lot of people and hear a lot of names. Sorry, I can't help you."

"That's okay. Anything new on the murders?" I ask.

She raises a perfectly styled eyebrow. Somehow I focus on her eyebrows every time I see her. What is it about them? Maybe I should have mine plucked to look the same. Maybe my subconscious wants perfect eyebrows. It might explain the inner restlessness I've been fighting all my life. Yeah, if only things were that simple.

"Shouldn't you be telling me?" She chuckles softly. "After all, I employed you to look into them."

"I meant, have there been further murders?"

"No, not that I'm aware. And I rescheduled our morgue appointment to after the congress. It felt like less of a priority after what you told me this morning. But don't get me wrong, I still want those responsible brought to justice."

"You may get both in one go. If they were killed by Fangs - or at least on behalf of them - their killers could be involved in the collar plans. I'm still not sure why they would make the murders so obvious and expose their insignia like that, but they must have a reason."

"What if it's a warning?" Gryphon muses. "From someone who isn't a Fang? Did you check if the people killed were sirens?"

"I don't know. I've never tried that. Usually, I find out if my targets are sirens before I kill them."

The mayor rolls her eyes. "Please, no talk of unsavoury things. Plausible-"

"Deniability," I complete the sentence. "We know. So let's just think what it would mean if they indeed weren't human. Why would someone leave a Fang coin on their corpses? It doesn't make sense unless..."

"Unless?" Lady Lara asks sharply.

"Unless they were Fangs and someone's killing them. That would mean there's someone out there who's got the same vendetta we do. But that's just a theory. One I like a little too much, so it's probably wrong."

"And they're leaving the bodies near the town hall to get the mayor's attention," Ryker muses. "Even if you, Lady Lara, didn't already know about the Fangs, you'd certainly investigate by now. Five corpses with strange coins, that would make even the most stupid humans investigate."

"Six," the mayor corrects. "Six dead people. They weren't anyone important, so I doubt they were at the top of the Fang hierarchy, if indeed they were sirens. Wouldn't someone interested in eradicating that organisation go for the people at the top?"

"I would," I agree. "But maybe they're not confident enough. Or this is their way of asking for backup. I don't know. Let's leave this for tomorrow and focus on the sirens on my list instead. Those are more concrete targets."

Lady Lara gets up, clearly showing us that this meeting is over. "Good luck. I'll reschedule that morgue appointment for tomorrow morning. If this isn't the work of the Fangs, I want to get more information before the conference."

I nod. "Please don't say 10 in the morning."

"10 am." She grins evilly. "Not a minute later. The coroner doesn't like tardiness."

"Phffffff. He can-"

"She. And she's a lovely woman. Now off with you, you've got business to do."

I love how she doesn't say 'you have people to kill'. No, she's all diplomacy and political correctness. I wonder if that's a skill she had to learn or if she was born with it.

"Well let you know how it went," I promise."

"Good, but this time, give me a call. No more nightly visits please."

I grin. "I can't promise that.

We split up as soon as we're out of the town hall. We've each got a target and an hour to get to them.

"Ready?" I ask, taking in each of my guys. They carry weapons, many of them, but an ordinary passerby wouldn't know. We blend into the crowd, even Ryker, who's wearing sunglasses. Luckily, it's a beautiful day.

"Check your watches. We need to strike at the same time."

Our clocks match. I'd already checked when we left the house, but it's always better to make sure. We don't want one of our targets to alert the others. We don't know if they're in contact with each other. It's not like we even know that they're all sirens. We're going in blind and I don't like it, but it's better than waiting. For once, we can take the offensive.

"I've got a cat assigned to each of you," Ryker reminds us. "Lennox, Gryphon, if you need assistance, rub the cat's head. If you're not going to be able to kill the target for some reason, rub their tail."

"What do we do if we simply want to cuddle the cat?" Gryphon deadpans.

"Don't touch their bellies. They don't like that."

I raise my hand. "I do. You can rub my belly any time you want."

Ryker's bright yellow eyes turn into fire as he looks at me with pure hunger. "Later," he says huskily. "Later."

Heat rises within me. That's a promise I'm looking forward to. But first, we need to kill some sirens.

A tiny tabby comes running over the square, meowing loudly until he's reached us. He rubs against Ryker's legs, his tail barely reaching my mate's knee.

"What is she saying?" Gryphon asks.

"He," I sigh. "Seriously, isn't that obvious?"

"Not to me, no. It's just a cat. It's not like he's showing off his endowment to make sure everyone knows."

"Gryphon, no dirty talk about my cats," Ryker growls. "He's just talked to the cats who've been waiting at the four addresses. We're lucky, there are people at all four places. Of course, we don't know if it's our targets, but it looks promising."

I bend down to give the little cat a scratch between his ears. He purrs his thanks before running off again. I stand up tall, make sure my knives are still where they're supposed to be, and smile at my men.

"Let's hunt."

IT TAKES ME ALMOST HALF AN HOUR TO GET TO THE HOUSE. It's so far out of town that I'd barely call it part of Attenburgh. And it's not a house, it's a villa. It could easily be a hotel, with dozens of rooms and a massive garden spread out all around it. A row of young birch trees leads to the main entrance. Not quite a proper boulevard yet, but maybe one day. I don't take that route, obviously. I stay in the shadows, grateful for all the bushes and trees surrounding the mansion. There's no sign of Ryker's cats, but I'm sure they'll seek me out if they have something important to report.

Once I've found a large bush to hide behind - one of the few that doesn't have thorns - I close my eyes and extend my senses.

Thirteen people. Fuck. And most of them seem to be in the same room on the ground floor. That's not going to make things easy. It's not like I can wait until dark when they might disperse to go to sleep. No, I've got less than half an hour to get to my target unseen. And I need to make sure I've got a route out again as well. In the past, I would have been less careful about that aspect of the hit, but now that I have a family, I can't be as careless. I need to be back in time to feed the babies. There's no time to hide and wait it out.

I stay in that spot until I've gathered enough sensory information. Three people are apart from the main group. Two smell like food even from this distance, so I assume they're cooks or servants. Only one person is on the first floor, all on their own. I so wish that's my target. It's a woman, so that fits, but I doubt my luck is that good. The only way to find out is to enter the house.

My target's name is Rosalind Tailor. I have no idea who she is, but she must be rich. Mr MacFay knew her address by heart, which once again speaks for the fact that she's loaded and probably important. I wish I'd had more time to ask him for details, but this has all been a bit of a hurry. Maybe it's her house, maybe it's her family's. Either way, she needs to die in twenty minutes.

I run across the lawn as fast as I can towards a pair of

white patio doors. They're unlocked and I slip into the house unseen. That bit was easy. The crowd is at the other end of the mansion, but one person is moving towards me. I breathe in deep. Human. Male. Not one of the foody people. Maybe he's looking for the toilet.

I randomly choose a room to my right and walk into it before the man comes into view. The door creaks a little, but it shouldn't be audible for any non-shifters, not at that distance.

Turns out I'm in a broom cupboard. How lovely. Well, a bit bigger than a cupboard. It's the size of my bedroom, yet the only thing they use it for is storing cleaning supplies. What a waste. It smells of dust in here, paired with the sharp sting of bleach. I doubt I'll find anything useful in here.

I wait while listening to the male's footsteps. He's continuing along the hallway, right until he's outside my door. He smells human, but why am I starting to think he knows I'm here? I made sure to evade the two security cameras outside and I didn't spot any in the corridor.

He stops for a moment and I get ready to attack if necessary, but then he opens the patio doors and leaves the house. Phew. Not that I don't want to kill him, but I have other priorities. Once my target is dead, I can deal with the others. I stay in one place as he moves away from the building and into the surrounding gardens. Maybe he wants to have a fag or just needs some fresh air. Either way, for now, I can continue.

Halfway down the corridor, I stop and breathe in deep. I'm close enough now to figure out who's a siren and who isn't. And it's my lucky day. Nine sirens in one room. Bingo. That's going to be fun. Sadly, it also makes it harder to know which of them is my intended target. The woman on the floor above smells human, so I doubt it's her. Still, I'm going to deal with her first. As much as I cherish the challenge of fighting an entire room of people, I still have some time until the hit. I check my watch. Twelve minutes.

The stairs are covered in carpet, just like in the Delaneys' house. Must be some kind of posh trend. It helps with not making a sound, but I won't have my stairs carpeted any time soon. It's such a waste of material, but I suppose that's exactly what it's all about. These people are stinking rich and want everyone to know.

The first floor is very different from the one below. Instead of a dark corridor with lots of rooms on either side, this one has a large space around the staircase filled with statues and display cases. It reminds me of a museum, except that we're in a mansion, not a public building. Only two doors lead away from this room. The human female is to my left, but I can't resist looking at some of the exhibits first. This is not something I've ever come across in all my years of breaking and entering. Yes, of course I've seen expensive paintings and the occasional statue, but nothing on this scale. There have to be at least thirty display cases here, spread out around a space that's larger than my house. Crazy.

The closest display holds a single lock of dark brown hair. *The Wolf of Horton.* A wolf shifter? The glass is too thick for me to get a scent. Either way, it's weird. Why on Earth would you showcase some hair like that? I mean, it's hair. Come on. A tail maybe, or a paw, or even a large piece of fur, but not just a bundle of hair.

The next showcase is more interesting. A bronze goblet holding a light blue liquid. It reminds me of a poison, but again, I can't smell it to make sure. The brass sign beneath the glass is a little rusty, but I can just about make out the words. *The drink that killed Duke Fortingham. Fay Lip's Poison.*

Not a poison I've heard of before. I shall have to research it; it sounds enchanting. Never heard of Duke Fortingham before. May he rest in peace, whoever he was. It's very strange to show a poison used to kill some noble guy though. The next few display cases aren't any less bizarre. The claws of a bear shifter, a faded piece of linen that once belonged to a cult leader, and a wooden pipe with the inscription *The Piper of Hameln, father of sirens*. It's the cleanest display, clearly marking it as the one that gets the most attention.

Now we're getting somewhere. Father of sirens. I need to ask Gryphon about that. It's definite proof though that the people living here are sirens.

I look at my watch. I better hurry. I ignore the rest of the display cases - I can always look at them once everyone's dead - and silently walk to the door behind which the human woman is waiting for me. I don't tiptoe - that would upset my balance. It's something people only do in books. Real assassins walk on the whole sole of their feet to stay grounded.

Now that I'm closer, I can hear the sound of a pen scratching over paper. She's writing, which should mean that she's distracted. I shall have to be fast to stop her from screaming, but if my senses don't deceive me, she should be sitting close to the door.

I take a deep breath and centre myself, pushing away all distracting thoughts. It's time to be the assassin I was raised to be.

The woman never has the chance to react. I'm behind her in one fluid movement and have a hand on her mouth and a blade against her throat in an instant. She's in her early thirties, with hair styled upwards so it looks like she's wearing a small traffic cone on her head, and thick glasses that I think are just for show. She's sat at a desk laden with files and books. Maybe she's some kind of secretary or personal assistant. The office is massive, with beautiful large windows looking out over the gardens. I could imagine doing my admin work in here. It's a lot less claustrophobic than my own small office.

"Shhhhhh, don't try to scream or I'll cut your throat," I hiss. "I'm going to remove my hand to ask you some questions. If you make a sound, you're dead, got it?"

She nods just as much as she can with the dagger pressed against her skin.

"Good. Don't make me regret this."

That's just for show. I wouldn't regret killing her. She oozes arrogance and money. The golden bracelet around her wrist must be worth what some people earn in a year. Her expensive perfume makes my nose itch. And why the hell is she wearing an inch of makeup on her otherwise quite pretty face? I'm tempted to get a cloth and wash it off to see what she looks like underneath.

Slowly, I pull back my hand from her mouth. Urgh, now I'm covered in red lipstick. I'd much prefer it to be blood.

"What's your name? Do you work or live here?" I whisper, hoping she'll get the clue and won't reply in a loud voice. I'd hate to have to cut her throat before I've got my answers.

"Maryam. And I live here. This is my parents' home."

Her parents? But she's human.

"Rosalind Tailor is your mother?"

She nods, her eyes wide, tears pooling at the edges of them. Pathetic.

"But... wait, were you adopted?"

"How do you know? Nobody knows that," she whispers. I don't think her eyes can go any wider.

"You're not a siren. They are, am I right?"

She purses her lips as if she's deciding whether to reply. Ah, it's that moment where my victim decides to play brave. I flick the knife in my hand, twirling it so the light reflects in the perfectly sharpened blade.

"Tell me or I may have to make an example of you."

"Yes," she sobs, her tears now flowing freely. "My mother is, but my father is human. How do you know about sirens?"

"Are they part of the Fangs?" I ask.

Okay, now her eyes are about to pop out of her skull. What a silly woman. She should have realised by now that I know more than normal people.

"Are you here to kill them?" she whispers, sobs interrupting her words.

"Kill who?"

"The Fangs! They're downstairs with Mama, negotiating. She sent me away because she doesn't like it when I get too close-"

"Wait, she's not part of the Fangs? But she's doing business with them?"

"Not business. Not voluntarily. They force her to work with them, but she doesn't want to. Mama isn't like other sirens, you have to believe me."

I hate when they use that sentence. I don't need to believe anything and anyone. I make up my own mind, thank you very much.

"Are all the people downstairs part of the Fangs?"

"All but my parents, yes. They always come in a group. I don't think they trust us very much. Mama usually tries to keep me and Papa away from them. They don't understand why she married a human."

My mind is racing. Things are turning out to be very different from what I thought. Maybe I shouldn't kill Rosalind yet. If she's not working with the Fangs voluntarily, and if she's pro-human, then maybe we could use her for our advantage.

I check my watch. Five minutes. I need to get a move on.

"What does your mother look like?" I ask.

"You're going to kill her?"

"No, I need to know so I don't kill her." I sigh. "Quickly now."

"Grey hair with some black streaks. She's wearing a green dress and a diamond necklace. She usually has a crocodile-skin handbag, green like her dress. And she's got glasses, almost the same as mine. My Papa-"

"Your father's outside in the gardens. He's not with the others."

I assume that was him. He was the only human male who didn't smell like food, so unless he's been the one cooking today's dinner, he must be her father. Hopefully, he'll stay outside and out of the way until I'm done.

I quickly tie her up with some parcel tape from her desk, fixing her to her chair. She squeals when I put some tape over her mouth.

"Quiet," I hiss. "You don't want to alert them."

"Hhhmrpphhhhhffff."

I sigh and remove the tape just enough to let her speak.

"But they're sirens! They'll make you do whatever they want. You don't stand a chance."

I grin at her and put the tape back in place.

"You have no idea, sweetheart. Wait and see."

CHAPTER SIXTEEN

I hate anti-siren tech. It gives me a headache. I'm not sure how exactly it works, but it seems to be some kind of soundwaves that mess with the sirens' ability to influence others. In this case, me. For that, it's worth it, although I'm going to switch it off as soon as I'm done. The little black box is secured to my belt and I swing it around until it's at my back, out of the way. I suppose if those sirens knew what it was, they could try and break it, but this portable tech is still new enough that I doubt they'd recognise it. I'd leave it outside the room if I knew what range it covers. I'll have to ask Benjamin next time I see him.

One minute to go. The door leading from the corridor to the large dining room is open, so I'm pressed against the wall, just out of sight but ready to storm in. I pluck some poison darts from my collar. This will make it easier to deal with nine people at once. I assume that the lady of the house will attack me, not knowing that I don't mean her any harm... yet.

I count down the seconds, ignoring the chatter from

the other side of the wall. In three other locations across town, my guys will be doing the same. I breathe in the siren stink coming from the room. It's going to be satisfying to kill them, especially now that I know they're all Fangs. I think back at what they did back home, poisoning children. There's no hesitation in my soul. They're going to die. No mercy.

The two humans have moved away from this room, probably to the kitchen. I hope they'll stay there; I don't want them to get in the way. There are nine sirens in that room.

Twenty seconds. I have four darts in my hand, but I'll likely only have the time to throw two or three before they realise what's going on. I've not had a lot of practice recently. Still, that'll mean three people out of commission, leaving only six to fight at once. If they're normal sirens, they'll have no fighting skills so it shouldn't be too difficult, even though I'm outnumbered.

Five. Four. Three. Two. One. Death.

I step into the doorway and throw my darts. The first hits an elderly man right in the neck. His hand goes up in a feeble attempt to get it out, but he crumples to the ground before he can ever touch the dart. The second grazes a woman's cheek. Hopefully, she got enough of the poison. The third embeds itself in a large man's throat. Good. I didn't have the time to decide who to dart, otherwise, I would have chosen the three strongest people in the room. This was pure reflex, throwing the darts at whatever target seemed most ideal. By the time I throw the fourth dart at a tall thin man wearing a top hat, the sirens have realised what's happening. A very fat woman pushes the man to the side, but my dart still hits him in the chest. His shirt is thin silk, offering no protection. The poison enters his bloodstream just like intended and a second later, he's on the floor. The overweight woman screams and glares at me. She opens her mouth as if to start singing, but I don't pay her any attention. She's not the greatest threat in the room, not with my anti-siren tech protecting me from her enchantment.

Two men are racing towards me, both looking strong enough to maybe have some sort of fighting skills. I don't wait to find out. I pull out one of the lighter throwing daggers and flick it at the man on the left. It slashes into his throat and he staggers back, his hands wrapped around the bleeding wound. Then the other man is upon me and I only just have time to grab my larger blade. He tries to kick at my legs, but it's an untrained move. I grab his foot and twist, getting him off balance. He stumbles, falls, and I jump on his chest, cutting his throat before he can even scream.

Three women have started chanting in the background, one of them Rosalind Tailor. She stands with the Fang sirens, but I guess she doesn't know that I'm not here to kill her. Probably. I could still change my mind.

A strange tingling sensation is running down my back, but the device at my belt seems to be doing its job. Their faces are contorted with effort, but I leave them be and focus on the remaining people. I'm almost done. This is way too easy. Where's the challenge?

I turn to a woman wielding a chair. She's the one the dart only grazed. Seriously? She throws it at me, but I roll to my right and it ends up landing on a corpse on the floor. That's not how you treat your dead. I pounce at her, but before I have a chance to cut open her flesh, a shrill sound makes me want to cover my ears. Only years of training stop me from following the instinct. I manage to press my blade against the woman's throat, immobilising her, then turn towards the awful sound. It's one of the three women.

She's blowing a silver whistle. Does she think this will stop me from killing her?

A noise from far away makes me freeze. Rustling leaves, heavy paws on grass. She's called for backup. Shit.

Without looking at the siren beneath me, I cut her throat before throwing the bloody knife at the woman with the whistle. It embeds itself in her left eye, right where I intended, breaking through her eye socket and into her brain. She stares at me with her good eye, then slowly, as if in slow motion, falls backwards onto a table. The table cloth gets tangled up as she falls, pulling plates and cups onto the floor. I delight in the sound of shattering porcelain. It reminds me that this is fun. Not just a job.

The last two remaining women are clearly frightened, but that doesn't stop them from keeping on singing. Rosalind seems especially keen on overwhelming me with her siren magic. The pressure against my spine increases. Not sure how much longer the anti-siren tech will work. And I have new enemies incoming. I only have seconds before they'll be here. Time to deal with those women. I jump up, ignoring the corpses at my feet, and launch myself at the woman to the left of Rosalind. She's young, maybe my age, but her eyes are cold and her lips pursed in disgust. Sometimes, I hesitate before killing women my age, but not today. I slice my blade across her throat, but before it cuts deep enough, something grips my wrist. I look down, expecting to see a hand holding me, but there's nothing. Fuck sirens.

Rosalind continues her song, now sounding more confident, almost jubilant, and I realise it's her doing. She's broken through my defences and I didn't even realise. How is she doing this? They didn't manage it when three of them were singing together, but now she's succeeding all on her own. I reach for the anti-siren box on my belt and pull back my hand when something sharp cuts my finger. Fuck. It's damaged. That explains it.

The woman beneath me is buckling, trying to get me off her, but I'm way stronger, even with one of my arms not doing my bidding. Luckily, I'm still not under Rosalind's control and my other hand is free. I pull a second blade from its sheath and plunge it into the woman's heart. It's not as satisfying as cutting someone's throat - I like seeing blood splatter as much as the next assassin - but it feels good to hear that crunch.

Now only Rosalind is left. Plus at least five mutant shifters almost upon me.

"I'm not here to kill you!" I shout. "Stop it! I was only here for the Fangs."

Her eyebrows shoot up, but she keeps singing. Damn woman. I don't have time for this.

Footsteps sound from behind me and a man barges into the room, wielding a steak knife. One of the humans.

Urgh, I don't want to have to kill him too. He's just an innocent cook.

Luckily - well, kind of - that's the moment the first wolf crashes through a window, shattering it. Pieces of glass rain down on the floor, but my focus is on the mutant. He barely looks like a wolf. His snout is too large, with fangs glistening from a maw that seems to have more teeth than any animal should have. His front legs are longer than his hind legs, but both have sharp claws that can probably slice through flesh like a diamond blade. And this isn't the only one. A second jumps through the window, with three others outside. Fuck.

The only positive thing about this is that Rosalind stops singing and the human man flees, screaming like a roasting pig.

Time to get some backup. I whistle sharply, alerting

whatever cats are in the area. There should be at least one of Ryker's spies nearby. Then I shift, faster than ever before, just in time. The wolf mutant is bleeding from multiple little scratches, but it doesn't seem to bother him in the slightest. He growls and then he's upon me.

I let go of all thoughts and surrender myself to pure instinct. I counter his strikes, block his claws, even manage to get a bite in once or twice, but he's larger than me and he's not alone. The other wolves surround me, nipping at my feet, trying to get in on the fight. The wolf I'm fighting with seems to somehow hold them back, as if he wants to do this himself. Suits me.

I feint to the left, letting him expose his right side. My claws tear through his skin, cutting into his flesh, but he twists and burning pain bursts through my left hind leg. His jaws are clamped around it and he starts shaking his head from side to side, bringing me off balance. I yelp in pain and stop attacking his right flank. I try to get him off me, clawing at him, biting whatever I can reach, but he's stronger. Shit. I'm in agony and it's making me lost control. Aimless struggling isn't helpful.

I need to be stronger. I've done that before. I pulled on strength I didn't realise I possessed. I need to do it again. But how?

More pain shoots through me, this time originating at my tail. I turn around just in time to see one of the other wolves rip off part of my tail. It doesn't seem real. The pain is real, certainly, but I can't understand how there's part of my tail in his mouth, no longer attached to my body.

Blood streams from the wound.

He fucking bit off my tail.

I go crazy.

· · ·

THREE WOLVES ARE DEAD ON THE FLOOR BY THE TIME backup arrives. I'm also barely conscious. My vision is blurred but I just about make out Lennox flying through the air, landing on one of the remaining mutants.

I trust him to handle those two. They're both injured, although I've lost track of how much. I'm covered in blood, both theirs and my own. It smells delicious, but I'm too tired to even start licking my fur. I sink to the floor, curl up and try to stay awake. I want to help Lennox, I do, but I simply can't. My energy is spent and I'm still bleeding from my tail and other wounds. There's a big gash on my belly where one of the mutants tried to rip me open.

Time passes. Blood flows. I'm slowly healing, but not everywhere.

"What were you thinking, taking on five mutants at once?"

Lennox has shifted back to human and is kneeling by my side. I didn't even realise he'd approached. I'm in really bad shape. And here I was full of confidence that I'd be able to deal with this on my own. And I was, until the mutants came. They were bigger and meaner than the ones in the forest. Those were easy prey. The ones today, not so much.

I meow softly in response to Lennox's question.

"Can you shift back?"

I slowly unfurl and look at my tail. The lower third is still missing. Is it going to grow back? I've never lost part of my body before, so it's hard to know.

"Fuck," Lennox exhales. "They bit off your tail."

I roll my eyes as if to say, thanks for letting me know.

"Maybe don't shift just yet. Who knows what part of you may be missing if you do."

I hadn't thought of that. I obviously don't have a tail when I'm human, so does that mean something else will be cut off? Some fingers? An ear? My boobs? Damn, he's made me a little scared. Or maybe more than a little, not that I'd admit that.

"I was done with my target within seconds," he continues. "He swallowed a poison pill before I could interrogate him. I left him in his house and decided to join you since you were closest. Glad I did. When the cat came running to fetch me, I thought the worst."

A little meow comes from behind me. I barely sense the cat standing there. Everything is dulled like someone's thrown a thick blanket over me. I want to sleep, but I know that's a bad idea. I've got so many things to do. I need to question Rosalind. Where is the siren? Was she killed?

I lift my head, groaning at the exertion. Fuck, that hurts.

"Stay still until you're healed," Lennox warns but I ignore him. I turn to where I last saw Rosalind standing, pressed against the wall. She's no longer there. Of course, she isn't. That would have been too easy.

"Cat, find the siren and her human daughter," I order to the kitty behind me. I can't smell her scent, don't know who she is. "They mustn't leave the house."

The cat meows and runs off.

"Should I follow her?" Lennox asks. I nod, then let my head sink back to the floor. I'm so tired.

Maybe a nap isn't such a bad idea after all.

I let darkness wash over me, removing all worries of missing tails and missing sirens.

CHAPTER SEVENTEEN

My boobs are still there. So are my ears and fingers. I run my hands over my body, searching from top to bottom to see if anything is missing.

"All there," I report to the guys.

"Thank the moon," Lennox sighs in relief. "Let's see if your tail has grown back next time you shift."

We're all in the Tailor mansion's living room. Lennox and Gryphon have pushed the bodies to the side, but they couldn't do anything about the carpet that's wet with blood. Ryker and his cats have found the Tailors, all three of them, and have brought them to us. The daughter - I don't even know her name - is the calmest, surprising me. She's got red marks around her mouth where the tape had stuck to her skin.

The human male, her father, is on a chair, looking very pale. His wife stands behind him, her hands on his shoulders, both to steady herself and to reassure him. She's covered in blood, just like the guys and me. We're all going to need a shower before we leave this house or we're going to cause a riot out there.

Gryphon hands me a glass of water. "Drink up. You've lost a lot of blood."

"I'm fine."

"You're pale as a ghost. Drink. I'm your doctor and you better do what I say."

I grimace but down the water as instructed. It feels good to wash the taste of blood from my mouth. As much as I sometimes like licking a bit of enemy blood, right now I want to concentrate on what's more important.

"Why did you leave your target alive?" Ryker asks and takes a seat on the floor next to me. He gently strokes my hair. I want to purr, but it doesn't look good doing that in front of our prisoners. That's what they are, I suppose. Until we know more, anyway.

"Because she may not be working for the Fangs voluntarily," I say, my voice hoarse. "I wanted to find out more before I decide whether to kill her."

I'm fully aware that they can hear me, even without supernatural hearing. The man sucks in a breath, but both women stay silent.

"Well then, let's find out," Gryphon says and claps his hands. "I've got other things to do, like looking after my mate and making sure she doesn't overdo it with those injuries."

I growl at him. "Your mate's just fine. Help me up."

"Oh no, you don't. You stay there until I give you the all-clear. You're still healing. Now drink more water."

"Water isn't exactly medicine."

He raises an eyebrow. "It isn't? Oh my goodness, that means my entire medicine degree was for nothing!"

I can't help but laugh at his dramatic antics. He can be adorable when he tries to cheer me up. Not that I need any of that. I'm happy now that I've had some kills, my boobs are still intact and I'm about to interrogate a siren.

"If I'm not allowed to get up, then at least bring those people closer to me," I demand. "It's hard to look menacing from the floor."

"The blood on your clothes makes you menacing enough," Lennox whispers. "Do you want me to threaten them a little?"

"Nah, they've just experienced a battle with mutant shifters. I think they feel threatened enough already."

The human male groans as if to say that I'm right. He's shaking and the only thing that seems to stop him from completely freaking out is his wife's firm grip on his shoulders.

Gryphon escorts the two women to me, pointedly ignoring the human. He makes them sit on the floor, something I'm sure they've never done before in their lives. Rosalind's pretty dress is torn in places and stained with various body fluids. Mostly blood but I'm pretty sure there's other stuff on there too. Her daughter has escaped relatively unscathed and she looks the most confident of the three. It surprises me a little, given her earlier hysterics upstairs.

I turn to Rosalind. "My name is Kat and I'm an enemy of the Fangs. If what your daughter says is true, so are you."

"Enemy," she splutters. "No, not an enemy."

"Mum," her daughter interrupts. "None of them are left to listen. You can tell the truth."

Rosalind looks me straight in the eye and I see some steel in there, a strength hiding behind pretty dresses and formal etiquette. She was the one who kept singing, I remind myself. She stood there and kept fighting even when everyone else was dead. Maybe she could make a good ally.

"You can trust us," Gryphon suddenly says. Of course,

he's a siren. They might trust him more than me. "I'm not a Fang even though I'm a siren like you. Some of us have left the families in protest of what's happening. You're not alone in wanting no part in it."

Rosalind looks at him for a moment, then sighs. "Yes, I'm not exactly friends with them. All my life, I've tried to run away from my heritage. I married a human against my family's wishes. At first, they banished me for it, cut me off, but I made my own fortune, built my own life. Then they came, seeing what I'd become, and wanted me back. They wanted to profit from the influence I have, the trust I've built with the human community. When I refused, they threatened me, my family."

"The Fangs or normal sirens?" I ask.

She laughs coldly. "There are barely any sirens left who've not joined the Fangs. They don't take no for an answer. I'm not proud of giving in to their demands, but I also won't apologise for it. They threatened my family, so I did what I had to."

"We understand," Gryphon says gently. "We've seen the things they do."

"You have?" Again, she laughs. "I doubt you know the full extent of their plans or you wouldn't have killed them all. Their revenge is going to be terrible."

Her husband gasps from the other end of the room where he's still sat next to an overturned table. Rosalind turns to him and gives him a tense smile. "Don't worry, darling, I won't let anyone hurt you or Sinéad."

Now I finally know the daughter's name. She stares her mother down as if she's angry. Huh. Curious.

"I don't need your protection. Haven't I proven that in the past weeks?"

Rosalind's expression softens. "Yes, you have. But maybe keep that quiet or you'll be in even greater danger."

"What?" I demand. "What have you done?"

Sinead looks at me, her entire demeanour suddenly changed. Gone is the immature, frightened woman. Instead, her eyes have become diamonds, a little rough yet ready to cut whatever gets in her way, and her posture is one of confidence and strength. Interesting. She's an actor.

"I have killed Fangs," she pronounces, eliciting a groan from her mother. "I killed them like they've killed humans. Like they threatened to kill my father."

Several jigsaw pieces flutter excitedly in my mind before coming together, forming a complete image. "And you left Fang coins on their corpses as a warning for other Fangs."

A tiny flicker of surprise shows on her face before her mask slips into place again. "Yes. You know about them?"

"I was asked to investigate the murders. My client thought it was the work of the Fangs rather than the opposite."

"And you didn't figure it out?" she asks with a disdainful smile.

"I haven't even seen the bodies yet," I hiss. "I had no idea that they're sirens. I got a little distracted by killing mutant shifters in your living room, in case you didn't notice."

"Who wouldn't have come here if you hadn't appeared," Rosalind says. "I've never seen them in action. There were rumours about them, abominations stronger than any other being, but I thought they were just that, rumours, created to intimidate us." Her gaze softens a little. "Are you very hurt?"

"I'll be fine." Embarrassment rises up in me. I hate showing vulnerability in front of these people. Especially in front of Sinead. A human who's killed FIVE Fangs.

Ridiculous. I give her that, I totally believed her hysteric-stupid-human act earlier. I suppose she must have years of practice at it if she's been surrounded by sirens who believe humans are nothing but cattle.

"How did you do it?" I ask her. "How did they not enchant you?"

She grins triumphantly. "I'm immune. I was born deaf and only gained my hearing after an operation. It's what we think made me immune to a siren's song. Most aren't aware of it; otherwise I'd probably be long dead by now. The Fangs have grown careless. They know they're close to achieving their goals and they're no longer careful about not showing themselves. With lots of them visiting our home, it was easy to choose the ones that would be my next kill."

"Sinead," Rosalind admonishes. "You shouldn't talk like that. I don't want you to be a murderer."

"It's too late for that, mother. I am a murderer but I'm proud of it."

"Not a murderer," I correct. "An assassin. Nothing wrong about that. You're in good company."

Lennox raises a hand. "Assassin."

Gryphon does the same, grinning wickedly. Ryker just shrugs, staying quiet. He's killed, today even, but he doesn't see himself as a killer. I think in his mind he's simply behaving like the cat he was born as, hunting his prey and killing it in the process.

Rosalind seems shocked, but Sinead smiles. "I've never met an assassin before."

I laugh. "Most people only meet them once before dying. But now that we know you're not Fangs, we won't harm you. On the contrary, you're going to help us take them down."

"Will we?" Rosalind asks drily. "I don't think so. As I

said, they've threatened my family. After today, we're going to be even more in the spotlight. I'll be able to say that we survived by some miracle, that you thought we were dead, but I don't know if they'll believe it."

"Which is exactly why we have to fight," her daughter argues, her voice swinging with passion. "It's time to end this charade. I'm tired of tiptoeing around them, pretending I'm just a stupid girl who knows nothing of siren business. I'm ready to take revenge for what they did to you."

I look at Rosalind questioningly. "What did they do?"

The woman doesn't reply, so I turn my gaze to Sinead. She averts her gaze, clearly aware she's said too much.

To my surprise, Mr Tailor speaks up. I'd completely forgotten about him.

"They made us lose our child. They sang until it was dead. Said a siren-human-child didn't deserve to live."

Gryphon gasps. "They did what?"

Sinead looks like she wants to attack one of the corpses. "They stood around her. Sung one of their eerie songs. They killed the foetus. I was going to have a brother and they killed him."

A shiver runs down my back. It was bad enough that the Fangs killed shifter children back home, but they did that by proxy. They never got their hands dirty. And now they killed one of their own, a siren? Fuck them. It's time to put an end to them once and for all.

"You know what they're planning at the conference?" I ask.

Both women nod.

"We're going to stop them before they even have the chance. I've killed eight Fangs today. My mates have assassinated more. They're going to be on high alert now, but we won't let that stop us. Rosalind, you're going to provide me with names and addresses. Then we're going hunting. By the time the politicians meet, there won't be any Fangs left to put collars around the humans' necks."

Rosalind scoffs. "Even if I did give you names, you don't stand a chance. Look at you. You're injured. Your men don't look in the best state either. The Fangs you killed here today weren't the top dogs. Those will have security. They won't be easy targets and they're going to kill you before you even get close." She points at the little black box lying broken next to me. "That anti-siren tech? They're already working on a solution against it. They'll have warned their bodyguards to destroy them so that they can pick you off one by one. You don't stand a chance. No, you better pack up and leave town. That's your only hope of surviving."

"Mum," Sinead protests, but Rosalind motions her to be quiet.

"Sinead, this isn't a game. I've tolerated you going after those people because I knew they were harmless. And you didn't think you were out there on your own, did you? I always had people follow you, ready to step in if necessary. Your little assassin illusion ends now. We're leaving and if you know what's good for you, Kat, you will too."

I shake my head. I won't accept this. I need her on my side. She can give us names that would take us forever to find out. Yes, we could go through every one of today's Fangs' houses and search for information, but we don't have the time. We need Rosalind Tailor, as much as I hate relying on a siren.

"You're going to help us," I order her, my voice as sharp as my blades. "Because you want revenge. I can see it in your eyes. Look around you. Look at those bodies. All these people will no longer be able to force you to do things against your will. They're history. Why do you let them banish you from your home? You've made a life for yourself, you said so earlier. Don't leave all that behind. Fight and make sure no one is left to hurt you or your family."

"She's right," Gryphon says, much gentler than I ever could. "Even if you flee, they'll find you eventually. You're used to a certain standard. If you want to live the same way, you're going to draw attention. And do you think you'll be happy, being on the run? Always looking over your shoulder. Always being ready to pack up and leave. Believe me, I've been there. It eats you up from the inside. You don't want that."

"You don't stand a chance," she repeats, but she no longer sounds as convinced. "How many of you are there?"

Lennox smiles, letting his wolf come to the surface for a moment. His eyes change colour, his entire presence transforms, showing the predator inside. "There's an entire wolf pack waiting for me to tell them where to go. We have assassins, thieves, poison experts. We're not alone."

"Wolf pack?" Sinead asks. "Wolf shifters? An entire pack?" She has a strangely greedy expression on her face as she runs her gaze up and down his body. "Do they all look like you?"

"He's mine," I snarl. "Now tell us where to find the Fang leaders. Most of all, tell me where Lord Delaney is hiding. I've got open business with him."

Rosalind looks me straight in the eye as if she's searching for something. After what feels like forever, she nods. "I'll make you a list. I don't know every Fang in Attenburgh, but I've done my research and should be able to give you the details of at least a dozen or so." She looks around the room. "After I've subtracted some of the people you killed here."

"I'll help," Sinead volunteers. "I may know some that mother doesn't. I made my own hit list, after all."

A meow comes from outside, anguished and full of alarm. Ryker jumps to his feet and I would do the same if I had the strength. Fuck this body. Heal, damn you. Don't grow back the tail if that means I can get up and fight whatever threat the cat is reporting.

Ryker turns around from the window, his face grave. "There's a fire. Someone set fire to our house."

CHAPTER EIGHTEEN

We run as fast as we can. Lennox and Ryker have shifted and have sprinted off, while Gryphon is by my side. Every movement hurts, but sheer desperation is driving me on.

My home is on fire. Are my babies safe? My siblings? Lily? Bethany? Benjamin? The kittens?

I can't even think of what may have happened. No, I push away my fears and run. I bump into people, not caring that we're drawing attention. I have to get home.

By the time we finally turn a corner to enter our street, the smell of smoke fills the air. A plume of it rises from the house at the end of the street. It's bad. The entire building is on fire. Flames shoot from the windows, all the way up to the attic. Humans have formed a circle around the house, watching and shouting. We push through the crowd, but don't get much further. Burning wood has fallen to the ground, blocking the front door. Sparks are flying through the air, landing on my clothes and my skin, leaving marks. I don't care.

"Lily!" I shout at the top of my lungs. "Caitlin!"

"We're here!"

Lily's voice comes from my right, behind a group of nosy humans. I run over, ignoring the pain in my limbs. Lily's on the ground, her face stained with soot. In her arms are Donna and Bella. The twins are awake but aren't crying. That worries me. They should be scared, right? Did they inhale too much smoke?

"Where are the others?" Gryphon asks from behind me.

"Benjamin is at the back, trying to get everyone out. I sent Lennox and Ryker to help them. Caitlin has Liat. Sophie's with her too. I sent them to find a phone and call for help. Although I'm sure one of the humans has called the fire brigade by now."

Yes, where is the fire brigade? How is it that we were faster running through half the town than for help to arrive? Fuck humans. They're going to let us burn.

"What about Bethany?"

"I don't know." Lily coughs. "It all happened so quickly. They threw something through the windows. There were explosions. I just ran to the nursery and grabbed the babies. I was trying to carry them all until Caitlin came to help."

"All the babies?" I sound hysterical but I don't care. "What about Shade? You didn't mention her! Where is she?"

"She was with Bethany before it all happened. They were in the kitchen, I think..."

I look at the kitchen window. Thick black fog rises through the shattered windowpane, interspersed with red flames.

Something inside of me stops. My baby. My beautiful little Shade.

Gryphon lays a hand on my shoulder. "We'll find her. She'll be okay. Can you sense her?"

"No, the smoke blocks it all." Tears spring to my eyes. "I can't smell her."

"Let's go to the back of the house, maybe she's there."

He kneels by Lily's side and kisses the twins on their forehead. "We'll be back."

I do the same, hugging my babies, breathing in their scent.

Bella mumbles something, half asleep.

"Shhh, stay with Auntie Lily. I'll be back in just a moment. Go to sleep."

It hurts my heart to turn away from them. It goes against every motherly instinct, yet I have two other babies out there. I trust Caitlin to keep Liat safe, even though I'd give everything to have him in my arms just now. I won't quite believe that he's okay until I've seen him with my own eyes.

I follow Gryphon, running around the house, evading burning embers. Roof tiles are falling down, crashing into the ground like missiles. One grazes my elbow but I keep running. It's not like I'm not in pain already. Every single muscle is screaming out in agony. All that keeps me upright is the fear for my daughter. It's amazing what love can do.

We climb over the garden wall to get into the backyard. It looks even worse here. The roof seems close to collapsing and every single window is lit by flames. Huddled against the stone fence are the Ryker, Lennox and Benjamin. A few cats are at their feet, but it's not all of the ones living in our house. Ryker is cradling a kitten, half its fur burned off. It's mewing softly, but it looks like it's just superficial burns. Benjamin is covered in soot and ash. Red blisters are all over his arms where he must have got too close to the flames.

"What's the situation?" I ask, trying to be as objective as I can.

Ryker faces me and I realise there are tears in his eyes. Fuck. I've never seen him cry before.

"Pumpkin ran in to save his kittens," he says in a croaky voice. Every single syllable is heavy with fear. "I tried to stop him but he was faster. He's such an idiot, running into a burning building..."

"You tried to run in after him," Lennox points out quietly. "And you would have succeeded if I hadn't tackled you to the ground. You're no good dead to your son or any of us."

I take Ryker into my arms and press him as close as possible without squashing the kitten. He smells of fire, just like all of us by now. I don't know what to say. Is there hope for Pumpkin? He's small, but the entire house is on fire. I can't see how he'd get out alive, let alone save the other kittens. Some of them are injured, which is why they're staying here under his care and leadership. He's become a mini-Ryker, collecting cats and adding them to his own little family.

"He'll be alright," I whisper, hoping I'll sound convincing. "He's strong and clever. He'll find a way out."

Ryker doesn't say anything. He simply presses his face into my shoulder, burying his head in my hair. As if he wants to hide from reality. I get it.

"Benjamin, did you see Shade?" Gryphon asks urgently. "Lily said she was with Bethany."

"I don't know." Benjamin coughs. "I know she was in the kitchen half an hour ago, but she may have been somewhere else when the fire started. Bethany was trying to teach Shade how to make simple poisons."

In another situation, I would have laughed at the idea of Bethany showing a baby how to create poisons, but this isn't the moment. I'll save that for when everything is okay again.

WITH RYKER STILL PRESSED AGAINST ME, I HOLD OUT MY hands. Gryphon and Lennox take them without needing me to say anything. I pull them close until we stand in a huddle, warming each other to dispel the icy cold within us even as the flames crackle with malice all around us. One of my babies is missing. I need to do something, but what? Running into the burning house is something my heart urges me to do, but I know better. The guys would never let me. No, she might still be alright. Bethany may have taken her to safety. If only this smoke was gone so I could sense her.

I never knew fire could be this loud. It's a strange roaring and crunching, like a beast devouring its prey. More roof tiles fall to the ground. Broken shards lie all around us. If I was a poet, I'd compare them to the pieces of my cracking heart. But I'm not. I'm just a mother hoping with every fibre of her being that her child is alive.

"What do we do?" I whisper.

"We ask the humans," Lennox suggests. "They may have seen Bethany and Shade. Right now, who cares that we may draw attention to Shade's fur. We've already got the attention of the entire street, no, this part of town."

A siren sounds in the distance. The fire brigade, finally. By the time they'll get here, the house will be nothing but ash and embers.

Another crash inside the house. It's falling apart. Then, a voice, a man. Huh.

"Help!"

I don't recognise the voice, but it doesn't matter. He's close, he must be just beyond the burning back door. I exchange a look with the guys. There's no way we're staying back now.

Gryphon rips off his shirt and wraps it around his hands before running towards the house. Lennox does the same and together, they manage to open the door. it breaks into burning pieces. Now that we can look inside, my heart sinks. It's nothing but flames there.

"Hello?" I shout. "Where are you?"

No reply. But then, a baby cries. I'd recognise that sound anywhere. Shade. Her voice is a little higher than that of her sisters. Gryphon always says that one day, she might be a soprano while they will be altos. Not that I care in this very moment. Shade's alive. And in a burning building, cut off from us by a wall of flames. The world has never looked this bleak.

Another crash. Then, a figure appears beyond the flames. The smoke makes my eyes water and it's hard to see, but it's definitely a man.

We need water to quench the flames, but the sirens are still too far away. Why aren't the humans getting buckets of water from their homes? Why is nobody helping?

"I'm going to try something. I have no idea if it works," Gryphon announces and stretches out his hands as if he's trying to hug the building. He opens his mouth and begins to sing. It's a calm, gentle melody, completely at odds with the inferno in front of us. It washes over me, soothing some of my fears. I don't want it to. I push it away and like always, Gryphon's magic isn't strong enough to fully enchant me. I turn to look at the others. All three men are smiling. Benjamin looks the most dazed. No surprise there, he's only human.

Gryphon's voice turns louder, the song stronger and more forceful. He's tried the gentle approach, now he's going to fight. The flames licking at the doorway quiver. At first, I'm not sure if it's just the wind, but no, they're responding to his music. Wow. I had no idea he could do that. From the surprised look on his face, neither did he.

Encouraged by this first success, he continues singing the flames into submission. They clearly don't like being stifled by the siren's song, but he's stronger. With every passing second, they grow smaller until they're nothing but sparks and smouldering embers. Gryphon steps forward and starts working on the flames between us and the man. Sweat pearls on his forehead, turning the ash on his skin into mud. I wish I could give him some energy - not that I have a lot left.

"Kat!" I whirl around to see Bethany climbing over the wall. Except for some scrapes, she's unharmed. And not with Shade. Anger boils up in me. As much as I'm happy to see that she's safe, my baby is in a burning house because Bethany didn't get her out in time. I trusted my friends to keep my children safe.

"There was a noise outside and I went to check," she pants, clearly able to read that I'm about to shout at her. "I left Shade in the kitchen; I didn't want to endanger her in case more grunts were out there, ready to attack. Just when I'd stepped out of the house, the explosions happened. I'm sorry, I tried to get to her, but I was thrown back and knocked unconscious, and by the time I woke…"

Her shoulders droop and she looks so lost and remorseful that my anger vanishes.

"Someone's got her," I explain, focusing back on the figure in the smoke. "Gryphon's trying to push the flames back so he can bring her out."

By the time the flames are finally low enough for us to see the man properly, Gryphon is wavering on his feet. Lennox is by his side, supporting him, while I try to stay standing despite the pain. Ryker hasn't said anything, hasn't moved. He seems frozen in shock and grief. I wish I could help him. I wish we'd heard Pumpkin's meow together with Shade's cry.

Gryphon's voice is getting quieter, but it's still having the desired effect. The flames retreat, giving a clear path between us and the man. He stumbles forward, clutching something to his chest. His face is hidden in shadow now that the fire no longer illuminates the room. He's got a basket in one hand, but he doesn't look like he's going to be able to hold it for much longer. The poor guy must have breathed in a hell of a lot of smoke. It's a miracle he's still standing.

I no longer wait. I run in until I'm face to face with him. Without a word, I hold out my hands and he passes me the bundle in his arms. Shade has been wrapped into a wet towel, although it's almost dry by now. She blinks up at me with wide eyes, then smiles. She's okay. I squeal, yes, I actually *squeal*. I kiss her, then hug her as close as I can without breaking her. For a moment, the world is fine again. Until the man next to me does a gurgling breath and drops to his knees.

Alright, maybe the world isn't quite alright yet.

I take the basket and am greeted by a meowing complaint from inside. So he's not only saved my daughter, he's also rescued the kittens. Who is this mysterious saviour? I never even looked at him; I was so occupied with making sure Shade was alive and unharmed.

I want to offer him my shoulder to lean on, but now Ryker joins me, staring at the young man. And I join him in staring, because the man - well, he's more of a boy - looks very familiar. As if he was Ryker's little brother.

"You need to come out, Gryphon can't hold it for much longer!" Lennox shouts from outside. Ryker grabs the boy and helps him walk, while I carry Shade and the kittens to safety. As soon as we're out of the house, Gryphon stops singing. He gasps for air, then sits down on the ground, pale and covered in sweat. He manages to smile at me though, showing me I don't need to worry.

I fuss over Shade, counting her little fingers and toes, making sure none of her black fur has been singed. Except for some soot staining her skin, she seems absolutely fine. It's a miracle. She smiles at me as if nothing has happened before wrapping her fist around my finger. I stroke her head, simply content with holding her in my arms. The kittens meow from the basket by my side, but they don't sound like they're in pain so I ignore them for now. They'll get some catnip later to help deal with the shock. I look at the burning house. Or maybe not. That's our catnip supply gone, along with everything else. Our home has gone up in smoke, literally, and it's still burning even now. On the other side of the house, the sound of water signals that the fire brigade has finally arrived. It's too late though. There's nothing to save. At least all of us are alive. It's just our home that's dead.

"Pumpkin," Ryker says and I realise I completely ignored him and the young man.

It takes a moment for the word to sink in. My mouth falls open as I stare at the boy. Dark grey hair. Skin the colour of my panther fur. Yellow eyes.

Ryker's eyes.

This boy is Pumpkin. The kitten has turned into a man.

CHAPTER NINETEEN

We make a sorry sight as we move through the streets of Attenburgh. We're using the same cart we arrived in a month ago, except that this time, I'm not bleeding with four newborns on my chest. We've put the kittens and the babies in the cart. Since we sold the horses, we have to push it ourselves. None of us has much strength left, but Gryphon is probably the worst for wear. His face has turned ashen and he clings to the cart for support. We offered him to ride on top along with the litter, but he didn't want to hear of it. He's proud, even at the verge of collapse.

Ryker and Pumpkin walk side by side, with Pumpkin coughing every few steps. He's breathed in too much smoke, but there's nothing we can do about it just now. I shoot them a look whenever I don't stare at my babies with gratefulness that they're still alive. Pumpkin is almost as tall as Ryker, but he lacks the bulk of his father. He looks like he's fifteen or sixteen, the kind of age where boys' limbs seem too long for the rest of their bodies. He's gangly, but that doesn't mean he's not pretty. I think most teenage girls wouldn't say no to him if he asked them for a date.

I've not talked to him yet, instead leaving Ryker to spend time with his son. It's hard; I'm brimming with curiosity. The kitten who started it all, without whom I'd never have met Ryker, just turned into a human. All this time we wondered if he'd ever be able to shift, but it took a life-or-death moment for it to happen. Just like with his father. The two of them look so similar that I'm having trouble picturing what his mother may have looked like. Maybe shifter genes are dominant over normal cat genes.

People stare at us, but I ignore them. We don't have a choice but to travel into the centre of town. Our home is gone and we need shelter. The sirens who torched our house - whether they were Fangs or not - may try to kill us again and none of us is in any position to fight. I'm slowly healing and the pain is abating, but that doesn't mean I'm ready to successfully defend my family against multiple foes. We need help, as much as it hurts to admit it. Our only hope just now is Lady Lara. I have no doubt that she'll give us refuge, even though it'll raise some eyebrows at the town hall.

Caitlin tried to call ahead, but she never got through to the mayor herself. When she called the fire brigade, they told her our house was blacklisted, whatever that means. It took her way too long to persuade them to send their people to deal with the fire. I'm going to have a word with whoever was in charge there today. *Blacklisted.* I do not doubt that Delaney or some other sirens are responsibly for that. They didn't want us to be able to save our home, our family. I don't know if they assumed that we'd all be in there. Either way, they're going to die, painfully.

Sophie joins me at my side and takes my hand. "I'm excited to meet her."

"Who?"

"The mayor. I've never met her but you keep talking about her."

I force myself to smile at her. "You're going to like her. She usually has biscuits in her office. I'm sure she's going to give you some."

"Chocolate biscuits?"

"Lemon, usually. Although I really wish she had catnip biscuits. I could do with some of those now."

Sophie nods enthusiastically. "Me too. Bethany should make them again."

"Did I hear catnip biscuits?" Lily calls from behind us. "That's very unhealthy!"

I look at Sophie and roll my eyes as dramatically as I can. "She has no idea."

"Have you ever told her to try catnip?"

"Yes, and she didn't like it. She said it tasted like parsley."

Sophie shoots Lily a disdainful look. "That's just wrong."

"I couldn't agree more. How are you feeling?"

"I'm fine. We got out before the fire got bad. Is that man truly Pumpkin?"

I nod. "Yes. If you get closer to him, you'll realise he smells like Pumpkin, even though he no longer looks like him."

My sister purses her lips. "I thought he'd be smaller."

"So did I. For such a small cat he's become a rather tall human."

"Do you know if he can shift back?"

"I hope so. Time will tell. For now, let's give him some time with his father. I'm sure they have a lot to talk about. Do you want to sit on the cart?"

She glares at me. "I'm not a baby. Maybe you should sit there instead."

I sigh. "Maybe I should. Don't tell anyone, but I'm exhausted."

"I won't," she whispers earnestly. "You can trust me."

"I know I can. And I'm glad to have you here with me. The next few weeks will be hard, but we've both been through much worse, so don't worry, we'll get through it."

I say it both for her and for myself. It's good to hear those words, even though it's me saying them. We'll get through this. We have to.

I LEAVE THE OTHERS OUTSIDE AND ENTER THE TOWN HALL alone. I don't want to scare the receptionist too much. But he isn't there. Instead, there is chaos. Police officers fill the lobby, looking grave and concerned. One of them, a young one barely out of puberty, stops me.

"Sorry Miss, you'll have to leave."

"I'm here to see the mayor. I'm her bodyguard."

He looks at me suspiciously. "You don't look like a bodyguard."

Yes, I suppose with all the blood and soot, I make a sorry picture. Not my best appearance, I give him that.

"Where were you two hours ago?" he asks me, his voice suddenly a lot less polite.

"Why?"

He grabs my arm. "Miss, I'm taking you to my commanding officer."

I don't have time for this. I grab his hand, twist and at the same time kick his legs from under him. He goes down with a shout of surprise. Yes, boy, I don't have much respect for your uniform.

I run to the elevator, swerving around police officers trying to grab me. I punch one of them in the face when he tries to get into the elevator just before the doors close. I use my knee to keep the door lock button pressed while holding down the secret key combination to let me take control of the elevator. Luckily, the police don't know about this and they haven't disabled the override. Once the lift starts going up, I lean against the wall, letting exhaustion run over me. Just a moment of not having to put on a mask of strength. If I could, I'd curl up on the floor and sleep for days. But I can't.

As soon as the elevator doors open, I stand up tall, pushing away my tiredness. People are running back and forth along the corridor, both town hall employees and more police officers. I'm starting to get a bad feeling about this.

"Judy!" I call out when a familiar woman hurries past. "What the fuck is going on?"

She's one of Lady Lara's assistants and even though I've only met her once or twice, she recognises me immediately.

"The mayor's gone," she says breathlessly. "She's disappeared."

I stare at her. My mind is taking a while to catch on to what she just said. "Gone? As in taking a surprise holiday? Or as in kidnapped?"

"We don't know but it looks like she didn't go voluntarily. There are signs of a struggle in her office. The police are looking into it now."

She reaches out to me, then thinks better of it and crosses her arms in front of her chest. "Can you look for her? I think you have a better chance of finding her than the police."

Huh. "Why would you think that?"

Judy steps closer and lowers her voice. "Because I think she wasn't taken by *people*."

Ah. She knows about sirens. Lady Lara must trust her enough to tell her about that.

I sigh and walk to the office, assuming she'll follow me. "Tell me everything you know."

JUDY FINDS AN EMPTY ROOM FOR US ON THE GROUND FLOOR and ushers my family in through a back entrance, unseen by the swarming police. They remind me of ants, running around in a strange pattern that may or may not have a purpose. It could well be that they're just trying to look busy while really not having a clue of what they're doing. If Lady Lara was taken by sirens - and it looks like it - then they can't do much anyway.

I sit on the most comfortable chair I could find and nurse Shade who's sucking so greedily that I can't help but wince. The guys hold the other babies, standing in line so they can get their lunch too. Or is it dinner? I've lost all track of time. Lady Lara's disappearance has filled me with enough adrenaline to keep me going, though.

Pumpkin and Sophie are in a corner with the kittens, using some wet towels to clean them. I still haven't had a chance to talk to Pumpkin. It irritates me and I blame the crazy world for it, but right now, I have other priorities.

The others have sat down, looking as exhausted as I feel.

"Benjamin, where's the fawn?" Caitlin asks quietly, almost a whisper. I get why she's doing that. The room is eerily quiet, with Bella's suckling the only noise. Even the other babies aren't making a sound. They must sense that something's changed.

"She ran out before the fire spread," he whispers back. "I didn't find her outside so I guess she must have run away. I hope she'll come back."

My sister puts an arm around his slumped shoulders. "I'm sure she will. That deer loves you."

Shade burps, telling me she's done. I look down at her, this little miracle with her big innocent eyes and fur-covered skin. I already got through having four babies during a battle in the middle of nowhere. This is nothing compared to that.

I hand Shade to Lennox and take Liat next. He's asleep but latches on as soon as I offer him my breast. He keeps his eyes closed while drinking. Adorable.

"Let's make plans," I say loudly. "We didn't get the refuge we were hoping for and our only chance to get help is to find Lady Lara. I don't think there's any doubt about who's taken her: the Fangs. I don't know why they did this instead of waiting for the congress, but it doesn't matter. We have to get her back. At the same time, we need to continue going after the Fangs. M.E.O.W. team, you don't know this yet, but the target I was intending to kill today turned out to be an enemy of the Fangs. They're going to provide us with names of every single Fang in this town. I'll call them as soon as I'm done feeding the babies. Lennox, can you call Mr Moon and let him know that we need his wolves to go after some of the less powerful sirens. Bethany-"

I suddenly realise something when looking at the poisoner. "The MacFays. Did they get out of the house?"

Her eyes widen in shock. "I didn't think of them," she whispers. "I didn't-"

"None of us did," Benjamin says, reaching out to her. "We had other priorities. Shall I go back and check on them?"

I think he means to check if they've burned to a crisp. I nod. "Do that and see if there's anything to salvage from the house. I doubt it, but better safe than sorry. Lily, Sophie, Caitlin, I want you to stay here and look after the children. You're going to be our nerve centre. We'll likely split up to reach as many Fangs as possible, and we'll call you whenever we have news. You can then relay that to whoever calls next. Good?"

Caitlin shakes her head. "Not good. I'm going to fight. I won't stay here like a child. You know I can fight. I was trained for it, just like you."

"But-"

"Let her," Lennox says and puts a hand on my shoulder. "She's right. We need every fighter we have."

"I want to come too!" Sophie insists. "I can-"

"No," I growl. "You're not coming. Caitlin is an adult and can decide if she wants to put herself at risk. You're not. We need you here as our point of call. Lily needs you."

"I do," Lily confirms earnestly. "I can't do this on my own, Sophie."

Before my little sister can protest further, I continue. "Bethany, do you want to fight or stay here?"

"Neither. I'm going shopping. We need medical supplies and food. I doubt you'll all return unharmed so I better get prepared. I'll coordinate with Judy. I might stop by the pharmacy and get some poison ingredients too. It won't be anything fancy, but if the sirens return to the town hall, we'll be ready."

"Good. Gryphon, maybe give Auntie Rose a call. If this goes pear-shaped, we may have to leave Attenburgh for a while. Let's see if she knows somewhere we could stay."

"I'm sure Mr Moon would put us up in his Pride house," Lennox says.

"Yes, but I prefer to be indebted to family rather than strangers with secret agendas. I like having Mr Moon as an ally, but I don't think our goals are totally aligned."

I turn to Pumpkin. "Will you stay here with the kittens?"

He nods. "I will."

Even his voice is so much like Ryker's. He sounds a little unsure, like he's still confused at why he can suddenly speak like a human, but he's dealing with it surprisingly well.

Ryker takes Liat from my lap and hands me Shade. "I'll alert the cats. They'll know about the fire by now and I don't want them to worry. If necessary, we can ask them to create some diversions near sirens' homes to keep our targets occupied until we have the time to kill them."

"Good. Does everyone know what they're supposed to do?"

Nods and quiet affirmations. While my guys leave the room, I continue feeding first Bella and then Donna while mentally making plans. I don't have proof, but I bet Delaney's behind the fire. We should have moved as soon as I got back from my kidnapping. He knew where we lived. Yes, we had installed defences, but they were clearly no good against explosives or whatever he used to set our house alight. It was arrogant to stay in our home. But I suppose we had other problems. Me being unwell, the babies needing a stable home. Stable-ish.

When Donna is finally done, I gently lay her on a blanket with the others and head upstairs to Lady Lara's office. There are still some police officers milling about, but less than earlier. Judy must have told them that I'm here to help, because this time, nobody stops me. They give me some curious stares but don't ask any stupid questions.

As soon as I enter her office, the smell of siren enters my nose. There must have been several of them for their stink to be this strong.

"Out," I snap at the two policewomen rummaging through Lady Lara's desk drawers.

"Who are you to tell-"

"Out," I hiss and bare my teeth. They make the right choice and hurry from the room. They'll probably fetch reinforcements but I don't care. I close my eyes and focus solely on my sense of smell. The more I concentrate, the more a picture emerges. The sirens came through the door, stopped at the desk, at least one touched the wooden surface. Then they left, but not all at once. One siren moved through the office, opening drawers and touching the shelves on the left. They must have been looking for something.

I open my eyes again. The leather desk chair is overturned, but I can't find any siren traces on it. Lady Lara must have pushed it over herself. That's the only sign of struggle. They must have overwhelmed her with their siren magic rather than physically. If they'd fought her, I would smell her adrenaline and sweat, but there's none of that.

I pull a chair next to the door frame and step on it to reach the anti-siren box screwed to the wall. It's hidden within a clock, but it seems that wasn't enough camouflage. It's been turned off. I give the clock a sniff. No siren touched it. A human. That means a siren must have enchanted someone to come in here and switch off the anti-siren tech. In theory, this box should counteract any influence a siren has on a human, but we never got to try if this is true for powerful sirens too. Gryphon refused to manipulate a human. Now I wish that he had. It seems it was possible after all.

I go back to the desk and righten the chair. It's just as comfortable as I remember. I pull a notepad from a drawer and get ready to call Rosalind Tailor when I spot a strange stain on the desk's polished surface. It's a wiggly line, ending in a splotch of ink. I turn on a light to take a closer look. *D-e-l.* Is it wishful thinking or is this the beginning of Delaney? Maybe Lady Lara tried to leave a message while she was taken. I would have gone to Delaney anyway, but this makes my conviction even stronger that he's involved.

Rosalind answers after only two rings of her phone.

"Do you have the names for me?" I ask before she can even say something. I'm in a rush, sue me.

"Yes. And Sinead has disappeared. I'm afraid that she's started going after them."

I sigh. Not another disappearance. "Are you sure she went freely?"

"Yes, her weapons are gone. She thinks I don't know about them, but of course, I do."

"Good, maybe I'll meet her on the hunt. How many addresses do you have?"

She dictates them to me. Some names are familiar. The locations are strewn all over town, although most are in the richer parts. Why can't all sirens just live in one large complex to make it easier to kill them? Can't they just do that one little thing for me?

The last name she says is Lord Delaney. I suck in a sharp breath. She's got his address. I won't have to interrogate other sirens. I can simply kill them and continue on to the next.

"Are you sure this is his current address?" I ask while writing it on a separate piece of paper.

"Yes, he's got two properties in town and I know his other one was attacked. You, I assume?"

"Most certainly. I killed his wife."

Rosalind gasps. "I'd heard rumours that she's dead but Lord Delaney insisted that she's simply feeling unwell. She was a half-siren, but of course, very few people knew that. Delaney would have killed anyone who said it out loud. It went against his whole philosophy."

"Call us if any Fangs turn up at your house. We're at the town hall."

I give her the number and hang up. It's time to hunt sirens.

CHAPTER TWENTY

I've torn the list of addresses into several pieces and hand them out to the guys and Caitlin. Lennox gets an extra large one since he'll pass on most of them to the Pride. Delaney's address is tucked away in my pocket. I've not told them that I know where he is. I want to deal with him myself. Yes, that goes against all the things they've tried to teach me, that they want revenge as much as I do, but I can't go against my nature. He's my prey and I don't share.

"Are you sure we shouldn't stick together?" Gryphon asks as he reads through his list. "We won't be as fast but it'll be safer. None of us is in good shape. This is dangerous, Kat."

He looks a little better, but he's still pale. I feel awful for sending him out to battle, but there's no time to rest.

"Okay, you pair up with Ryker. Lennox can join Mr Moon. By the way, do they have more anti-siren tech for us?"

Lennox shakes his head. "They need the few devices they have themselves."

"And all the tech we had here at the town hall has been destroyed," Ryker says darkly. "The door to the storeroom doesn't look like it was forced open, so someone must have had a key."

I nod. "The same someone disabled the anti-siren signal in Lady Lara's clock. They were either bribed or enchanted. Not that it matters now. We're going to have to be quick. Kill them before they even know we're there."

"I still don't think this is a good idea," Gryphon mutters. "Lennox should go with you."

"I can do this on my own," I hiss more forcefully than intended. "I'm feeling much better."

"This isn't about you being injured. It's about safety in numbers. Let's stop the lone wolf habit and work as a team."

No. Delaney is mine. "We'll discuss this later. We can do another intervention if you want. How to make Kat into a team player. Good luck with that. I don't care what you're doing or how you pair up, but I'm leaving. Call Lily whenever you're done with a target. She'll keep track."

With one last look at my babies, I storm out of the room. I need air. I need blood. And most of all, I need Delaney's head.

❖ ❖ ❖ ❖ ❖ ❖

THE HOUSE HE'S SUPPOSED TO BE IN IS A TALL BUT narrow townhouse in one of the poshest parts of Attenburgh. Its façade is freshly painted and the windows are so clear that they must be polished at least once a week. I don't know when our windows were last cleaned...not that it matters anymore. Our home is gone. Because of the arsehole living here in splendour while planning to take over the world. Not while I'm still alive. I wait around a street corner, out of sight from whoever may be in the house, and extend my senses. I'm tired and I don't get as much sensory information as I'd wish, but it's enough. The house is full of people. I hear at least eight different voices, but other noises speak of more inhabitants. The air around the front door smells like sirens, mostly, but I also sense mutant wolves. Just what I needed.

Delaney has drawn his forces close. He knows I'm after him. Maybe he kidnapped the mayor just to lure me here. Not that I care. Even if it's a trap, I'm going in there to cut off his stinking dick. He's not going to harm anyone ever again. My family will be safe. That's worth the risk.

I walk around the corner and leave the main street, sneaking along the path at the back of the row of townhouses. Most have small gardens, but not Delaney's house. He's got a shed instead. Probably where he keeps his torture devices. Who knows.

A man guards the back door, burly and most definitely a mutant. Probably one of those that can't die unless their head is cut off. Usually, I like the challenge they present, but today I don't have the time, nor do I want to arouse attention. There's no way I'll walk through the front entrance, so up the roof it is.

I use a neighbour's rose trellis to get me up the first third, then cling to the wall and climb using tiny gaps in the brickwork. It's hard work, but I manage to get up the roof with only a few scratches on my fingers. Those will heal within minutes.

Delaney's roof is more modern than that of his neighbours. He's got an attic window on either side, both of them new with double glazing. Maybe I should take over his house once I've killed him. He took mine, so I'll take his. But no, I need more of a garden, more privacy. I could set it on fire instead. Revenge served burning hot.

Of course, both windows are locked. It's not my lucky day, that much is for sure. I listen to sounds beneath, but the attic is deserted. I don't have any tools with me, so I shift my right hand and use my claws to cut through the plastic window frame. Should have invested in something sturdier, idiot. It takes a while and I almost break a claw, but then I'm inside the attic, crouched low and ready to act. I only have the weapons I had with me at Rosalind Tailor's place, and I left some of my throwing knives there in the hurry to get back home. It's not what I'd like, but it'll have to do. I still have one poison dart tucked away in my collar. It might come in handy.

A narrow spiral staircase leads down from the attic. The room beneath is empty too. Most of the noise comes from the lower part of the house, although there are three heartbeats on the floor under me. I don't think any of them are shifters; their heartbeats are slower than sirens'.

I sneak down the staircase to find myself in an empty room. Not even a shelf. Maybe this house isn't used very often. Delaney and his family had their home in Parseldon plus the other Attenburgh mansion, so who knows why he needed a third. Probably to make himself look even richer. Someone's standing outside the door, breathing heavily. I pluck a knife from the sheath attached to my belt and ready myself. Once I kill whoever's waiting here, I won't get another moment to breathe. Am I ready to do this?

I do a quick scan of my body. There are still patches of pain, especially in my shoulder where a mutant bit me, but I'm healed enough to fight. I won't be as fast as I usually am, so I have to take that into consideration. And I better not shift. Who knows what state I'm in should I try that. Maybe my tail is still missing and the wound bleeding.

That's a problem for another time. Tailless or not, I'll assassinate Delaney today.

With a deep breath, I fling open the door and grab the person standing there, pulling them backwards. It's a woman, small and stocky yet muscular. A fighter. I run my knife over her throat. She does a weird squeak that echoes through the empty hallway. That's my moment of surprise gone. I drag her into the room, out of sight, but I can't do anything about the blood splatters on the white door frame.

"Help!" a shout suddenly sounds from my left.

Lady Lara.

I sprint down the corridor, my senses telling me that two people are waiting for me, and barge into the room at the end of it.

It's my lucky day. Delaney and Lady Lara in the same room. The siren is lounging on a red sofa, his legs dangling over the armrest. Lady Lara on the other hand stands in the centre of the room, stiff as a board, a sword in her hand. An actual medieval-looking sword that probably belongs to the knight's armour in the corner. Again, the room is almost empty except for that sofa, the armour and a coat of arms on the wall. Delaney should have a word with his interior designer.

"Lady Lara," I say. "Glad you kept Delaney here for me. I've got some unfinished business with him."

Even though I've only seen him twice - once when he forced me to kidnap myself and once when he fought me while I was about to give birth - his sharp features have been burned into my mind. His eyes shimmer with malice. He's not even trying to hide his hatred for me. Well, two can play this game. I stare him down and flash my teeth, letting my fangs grow just for a moment.

The siren chuckles, a sound so cold it reminds me of

sharp icicles. "So do I, little kitty, so do I. I see you survived the fire. Such a pity."

"Lara, step behind me," I tell her. "We'll get out of here as soon as I'm done with him."

"She won't do that, you silly girl." His eyes start to glow and the mayor turns her head to look straight at me. Her expression is vacant, her eyes glazed. She's under his spell. Not a surprise but also not what I'd hoped for.

"Stop the games and fight me like a man," I challenge Delaney. "Or is that all you can do, controlling puppets?"

He stays in his relaxed position on the sofa, not seeming to care at all about the weapons I hold.

"I can do a lot more than you can even imagine. Now fight. I want to see you kill your beloved mayor. I've not had proper entertainment in a long time - and sadly I never got to see you murder my wife."

"You don't care that she's dead?" I ask, mostly to distract him. I don't want to have to fight Lady Lara. How do I get her out of his control without harming her?

"Oh, I care. It's going to be hard to explain it to my associates. For now, they think she's ill, so hopefully, they won't be too surprised when she suddenly dies from her illness. I should thank you for disposing of her, though. It saved me the effort of doing it myself. She's been a thorn in my side for years. Without her, you wouldn't have had to get pregnant. It was her idea, after all."

"Are you the father?" I blurt out. "Are they your children?"

He stares at me, then laughs. "Oh, you're so sweet, little kitty cat. Why on Earth would I waste my precious seed on someone like you? My wife and I had a child and she turned out to be crazy. We didn't need more of that. No, we gave you an experimental treatment, way too complicated for you to understand."

"Who's the father?" I repeat coldly. I hate that he knows more than me. He's dangling the answers over me like the proverbial carrot and the only way I can reach them is with his help.

"You'll figure it out, in time. But no, you won't. You'll be dead in a couple of minutes. So maybe I should tell you. Shall I?"

"Do it," I growl.

"There is no father. We spliced your genes, messed around with them, just to see what would happen. We never expected all four eggs to survive. They're abominations, nothing else. Now stop wasting my time and fight. It's what I've called you here for, after all."

Lady Lara gasps and raises her sword. She's not holding it the way she should, but I don't doubt that she could do serious damage with it. I need to disarm her before she gets the chance to hurt herself or me.

I sheathe my knives to make sure I don't injure her by accident. then dance around her, trying to get her from behind. She's fast, though. I don't know if Delaney's influence is helping with that or if she's simply a natural fighter, but her footwork is surprisingly good. She swings the sword in wide arches and I keep having to jump back to evade the blade. It glistens in the evening light streaming through the window, warning me that it's freshly sharpened.

"Lara, snap out of it," I growl. "You can do it. Fight him, not me."

Delaney laughs. "She's too far gone. With all that sneaky technology out of the way, she was easier to overwhelm than I thought. Would you like to know what she thinks about you? I can make her tell you."

I've had enough. In one fluid movement, I pull a

dagger and throw it at him. It's not a throwing knife, but it flies true, right towards his heart.

Until it stops. It hovers in the air mere inches from his chest. I stare at it, not quite believing what I'm seeing. Did he just use his siren powers to stop a knife in mid-flight?

A sharp pain bites through my right arm. Fuck. I let myself get distracted. Blood now coats the mayor's sword from where it cut my arm. It's a deep wound. I flex my arm. Thank the Great Cat, she didn't hit a tendon. It won't inhibit me too much. I take a few steps back until I'm almost at the door to get out of reach of that wicked sword.

Lady Lara's expression has changed a little, like a light has been lit in the darkness of her glazed eyes. Maybe she's trying to fight him, deep inside. I don't know what it must feel like to be completely controlled by a siren, but I know that she's strong, the strongest woman I know, despite being only human. If anyone can break that spell, it's her.

She approaches, swinging the sword again. This time, I duck, then dive under her sword arm and at Delaney. The only way to free her is to kill the man controlling her. I reach for the knife still suspended in the air, intending to push it forward into the siren's heart, but as soon as I touch it, it shatters into dust. Silver particles rain down to the floor. I stare at what once used to be my knife. What the fuck. This shouldn't be possible.

A movement in the corner of my eyes is enough to make me roll aside, just about avoiding the sword's deadly kiss. It almost seems like Lady Lara is getting better at wielding the blade. I need to finish this fast. I hate to do this, but I'll have to knock her out. Delaney won't be able to control her while she's unconscious. I hope. I'm starting to doubt everything I thought I knew about siren powers. I was aware that he's powerful, but I had no idea how much so. I'm going to mourn that knife later. It was one of my favourites. Yet another thing he's taken from me.

I face her, feign to the right and she follows the movement, while I twist around just in time. I punch her, my fist kissing the side of her chin right where I wanted to. Her head flies back, knocking her brain around. Just like intended, her eyes flutter shut and she collapses. I catch her before she touches the floor and gently lower her down. I don't want her to wake up with bruises all over. She's going to be confused enough already.

I only have a few minutes until she'll regain consciousness, maybe even less, so I need to make it count. I pull my remaining larger dagger and a smaller knife that was attached to my boots and focus on Delaney. He seems surprised but still hasn't had the decency to get up from the couch. He simply takes a whistle from his breast pocket and calls for backup. I cringe at the sound, but I don't let it phase me. This is my only chance. Instead of jumping him, I proceed a little more carefully, just in case he does some weird knife-destroying-magic again. Only when I'm two feet away from him do I swing my blades and attack.

Suddenly, my vision goes black and I can't help but stop in mid-motion. No, I can't let this stop me. It's another one of his tricks. I stab where he was sitting, but my knives only find air. I start swinging them around, stabbing and slashing, but even though I can still smell and hear him right in front of me, he's not there. What is he doing now? Is he messing with my head? He must be. I don't have any anti-siren tech on me, but it doesn't feel like anything it's felt like with Gryphon. With him, I knew that he was trying to manipulate me, a tiny voice at the back of my mind. That voice isn't here now. Even with my vision gone, I feel like I can rely on my senses - but apparently, that isn't the case.

Delaney has turned into a ghost, but I don't think the mutants running up the stairs will be as translucent. They'll be out to kill me and here I am, blind. This won't do.

"Delaney!" I shout. "Stop being such a coward and show yourself."

"I'm right here," he whispers in my right ear. I whirl around and stab where he should be, but of course, he isn't there. I don't know if he's playing with my mind, giving me wrong sensory information, or if he has actually managed to turn himself unstabbable. Either way, I've got a problem.

Lady Lara groans just when the first mutant crashes into the room. Not a wolf, but a man. Hello, trouble.

CHAPTER TWENTY-ONE

With the mutants at least, my senses seem to work correctly. I listen to their heartbeats, smell their sickly sweet scents that remind me of decaying apples, feel the shift in the air that their movements cause. And I attack. Desperation gives me new strength while anger gives me stamina. I need to kill them before I can get to Delaney. I won't let him get away again.

These mutants are so big that they're surprisingly easy to fight. My knives are slick with their blood as I stab and stab, almost always hitting flesh and bone. It's a new way of fighting but I'm surprisingly good at it. Yes, they get in a hit from time to time, but I'm nimble enough to dance away before I get serious injuries. My arm is still bleeding from where Lady Lara cut me with the sword, though. Luckily, the room is so empty that I don't have to think about crashing into furniture. The only obstacle is the mayor, but she's groaning enough to let me know where she is. She seems to be in pain. I hope I didn't break her jaw. Punches to the chin are one of the best ways to knock out an opponent, but it does carry the risk of damage, like any physical assault.

Stab. Slash. Stab. Evade. And again. It's a rhythm that only gets interrupted when one of them goes down. I don't know if I need to cut off his head to keep him dead, but I that would need too much of my time. Stabbing my enemies at random is fairly easy even without my vision, but finding their necks to sever their heads from their bodies is hard.

Two more mutants enter the room and circle me, trying to surround me. I dance back so that the wall is behind me, giving me at least some protection against surprise attacks. One of the new arrivals is devilishly fast. He knocks one of my knives from my hands before I can even counter his attack. Fuck. How am I supposed to find my knife without patting the floor for it like an idiot?

I feel the shift in the air just before he strikes and I manage to evade him, but only just. His weapon cuts my ear lobe and a strand of hair slowly drifts to the floor. Well, I was going to get a haircut anyway. Think positive. This isn't lost yet.

While I'm fighting the mutants, I'm aware that I should also be trying to fight Delaney's grip on my mind. But how do you fight something you can't even feel? There's nothing to push out. My mental barriers seem intact. I have no idea how he's doing it and that makes it even worse. It's an invasion I can't defend myself against. But there has to be something I can do. I refuse to give in to him. I know I won't be able to fight the mutants forever. There are more downstairs, just waiting for their turn. As soon as I cut one down, another will take his place. The only way to end this is to kill Delaney.

Which is impossible.

I growl and the sound of it reminds me of one other

option I haven't tried yet. I can shift. I don't think it's a good idea, not with the tail problem, but it's better than to die fighting blindly.

With a deep breath, I jump back as far as I can to give myself a second of extra time, then I shift. It hurts like hell. Every bone in my body aches under the strain, but luckily, the shift doesn't take long. Just when one of the mutants reaches me, I open my maws to rip out his throat. And yes, I can see him.

Fuck, yes. I'm no longer blind. And I feel stronger than ever.

I hiss at the mutants, warning them that playtime is over. Then I attack.

The world becomes a whirlwind of blood and death. I'm feral, driven by instinct. They don't stand a chance. I bite, claw, hiss and when one of them falls, I even purr a little. it becomes a dance that doesn't seem to have an ending - until a cold voice cuts through the rhythm.

"Stop or she dies."

I throw the wolf I had between my teeth aside - and only now realise that I've been fighting not just men but wolves too - and glare at Delaney. He's finally reappeared and he's holding a knife to Lady Lara's throat. Not just any knife. The blade I saw crumple into dust. Impossible. And yet there it is. Do I want to risk it being an illusion? No, I can't. I don't doubt that he'll kill the mayor if he's forced to. She's nothing but a pawn to him. If he can't control her, he'll control her successor. Humans are exchangeable for him.

But not for me. Well, not her, anyway. Lady Lara is special.

I growl at Delaney, flashing my bloody fangs at him.

"What happened to your tail?" he mocks.

I can't help but turn my head and look. I never had the

time while fighting, but now that the mutants stand still, waiting for their master's command, I can dare to take a look.

I suppress a groan. Half my tail is gone. It's no longer bleeding and new fur has formed where the wound used to be, but that doesn't make it any less sad. What's a panther with half a tail? Miserable.

"Now give up and let yourself be killed. I'll keep her alive if you do."

I scoff, as much as a cat can do such a human thing.

"Do you put your life above hers?"

No, I don't. But I don't intend for him to kill her nor me. We'll get out of here alive.

"Just let him do it," Lady Lara whispers, her face distorted with pain. She's no longer under his control, but he must have done something else to her. That or it's the effect of my earlier blow. Guilt courses through me. It was necessary.

I roar, showing her exactly what I think of that idea.

"Why do you keep fighting?" Delaney asks, his voice like honey rather than ice. "Why don't you just give in? It's tiring, isn't it? I keep besting you. You'll never win. I am stronger than you and you know it. You're our creation. We would never have allowed one of our creatures to be stronger than us."

I shouldn't be surprised that the Fangs were involved in the Pack's experimentation. He had Sophie, after all. Still, hearing him call me a creature doesn't do him any favours. I snarl at him as loud as I can. To my delight, he does step back before he catches himself. It's instinct. I'm a predator and he's the prey, no matter how much he pretends not to be.

I run through my options in my mind. There aren't many. Most of them end with Lady Lara dead. But that can't happen. I'd be the worst bodyguard ever if I let her be killed on my watch. It's bad enough that she got kidnapped.

"Let him kill me, then end him," Lady Lara says, breaking my train of thought. As if.

"Don't," Delaney replies, glaring down at her. "I need her dead, not you. Well, you too, if you insist. But this isn't a game of bargains. You will do what I say."

Lady Lara looks me straight in the eyes and slowly lifts her hand, putting it on the knife's hilt, covering Delaney's bony fingers. She struggles a little, just enough to turn her body to the right. She's no longer covering Delaney's body. The knife is now pointing at the siren yet he hasn't noticed her intention yet. I know what she's planning to do. It's brave, incredibly brave, and yet I hate her for it.

"Thank you, Kat," she whispers and with one last look at me, she guides Delaney's hand with one last show of force, pushing it all the way across her own throat and onwards to Delaney's chest. It only pierces his shirt before he stops the motion, but I'm already in the air, flying at him, and then my paw hits his hand and drives the knife deep into his chest.

He looks at me in surprise, then down at the knife embedded in his chest. Then back at me. The expression on his face holds no pain, only surprise.

Since I don't have opposable thumbs - you never miss them until you need them - I angle my paw to try and turn the knife. It doesn't work, but it does cause him enough pain to make me happy. His death is coming too quickly. I never got to cut off vital parts of his anatomy, let alone torture and interrogate him.

To my relief, the mutants are staying back, simply watching as their leader slowly dies. He sinks to the floor until he's kneeling over Lady Lara's lifeless body. I kick him away from her. He doesn't deserve to be anywhere near her.

He cries out in pain as he falls forward, driving the knife in further. And then he dies. It's a simple moment of one last breath and one last heartbeat. Thoroughly dissatisfying. I snarl at him, but he's gone.

Urgh. There wasn't nearly enough pain involved. I wish I could resuscitate him to kill him all over again. He deserves it.

I glare at the mutants, challenging them. If I can't have more of Delaney's death, then I shall have theirs. But they don't run at me as I'd hoped. They turn and run.

I huff and look after them, listening as they run down the stairs and out of the house. It's as if Delaney was the only thing making them fight. Now that he's gone, they couldn't care less about me, even though I've killed several of them. Their bodies litter the floor. Once again, I'm surrounded by corpses. This is becoming a habit.

Downstairs, a few sirens remain. They're not clever enough to flee. I gently rub my nose against Lady Lara's pale cheek to say goodbye. I will mourn her later. For now, I have more sirens to dispose of.

I'M THE LAST TO RETURN TO THE TOWN HALL. LILY WAITS in the lobby, sitting cross-legged on the receptionist's counter. When she sees me, she jumps down and comes running. She takes one look at my face and spreads out her arms. I walk into her embrace, but I'm too numb to return her hug.

It should feel like a victory, yet the bitter taste of failure is weighing heavy on me. I'm tired, dirty and covered in blood. I lost a friend today. And I didn't dispatch my enemy in the way I'd planned to.

"Is he dead?" Lily whispers.

"Yes." Again, I get no satisfaction from the word. Yes, he's dead, but at what cost?

"Good. I knew you were going after him. I was about to send the guys but now you're here. And look at you. You're filthy!"

She laughs and strokes my back. "Don't worry, we'll get you cleaned up. The mayor's assistant has organised food for us, lots of it. Your mates are tucking in as we speak.

I nod, too dead inside to even reply. I just want to curl up in a corner and sleep. Forget about it all. And then cuddle my babies and forget about the world.

"What's wrong? It's not just exhaustion. Did you find the mayor?"

I step out of her hug and simply look at her.

Lily gasps and covers her mouth with her hands. "She's dead?"

Again, I nod.

"Delaney?"

Instead of an answer, I walk out of the lobby, ignoring the police officers and town hall employees giving me very suspicious looks. I need to be with my family.

ONLY WHEN I'M SURROUNDED BY MY MATES DO I FINALLY feel something again. The numbness gives way to bottomless grief. They stroke my hair as tears run down my cheeks, mixing with dried blood and soot. I don't try to hide my tears. I just let them flow. In their midst, I no longer feel like I have to hide my vulnerability. And even if I did, I lack the strength to keep up my mask.

Somehow, we end up in a shower. It's not big enough

for all four of us, but they take turns washing me, brushing my hair, even cleaning the blood from under my fingernails. I just let it happen. I'm not quite there. They tell me how successful they were, how they killed almost all the Fangs on the list, how we're safe now. It should make me happy. I wish I could celebrate. We deserve to celebrate. We're finally free. No more looking over our shoulder. No more worries. We can have a life now. Delaney is dead, the Fangs decimated.

Gryphon wraps me in a fluffy towel and pulls me to his chest.

"We're here for you. We'll always be here."

I look up at him. into his grass-green eyes that always remind me of a meadow on a beautiful day. They glow with love, with care. I can't help but cup his face with one hand and pull him down until his lips meet mine.

Something inside of me cracks, cutting through the numbness. Sunshine breaks through the clouds. I kiss him like I'm drowning, letting him pull me back into life. He wraps his arms around my waist, pulling me close, holding me in his arms. The others join us, surrounding me from all sides. Their touch erases the last traces of purralysis and I can breathe again. I kiss them, one after the other, savouring the taste of life.

Yes, we're alive.

We're together.

And this is only the beginning.

ONE YEAR LATER

"Happy birthday!"

The words echo through the garden as they're roared by everyone. This family isn't exactly known for being quiet.

Liat claps his hand in excitement while his tail is wrapped around my neck. He's got heavy, almost too heavy to carry for extended periods, but I love him too much to put him down. I used to be able to walk around with two or more of my children clinging to me, but that's over now, no matter how much they complain. They grow too fast, way faster than human babies. Some days, I wish they'd slow down so I can enjoy every single day of their childhood, but then I remember how nice it is for us parents to see them grow out of their nappies at record speed. They all use the potty now and Donna has even started using the proper toilet, much to the disdain of her twin sister. Bella prefers us doing everything for her, including cleaning her potty. That little diva is going to be the death of me.

Lily drops into a chair by my side and grins at me. "Great party, right?"

I know she's fishing for compliments. It was her idea. Together with Caitlin, she's put on the biggest party I've ever been part of. Turns out my family is big and if you put us all in one place, it's kind of overwhelming. Luckily, our new house has a big garden. Lily has put up a pavilion to cover the buffet, just in case it starts to rain, but the weather couldn't be better. The sun is slowly setting, painting the surrounding forest in warm light.

"You've done well," I admit. "The kids are loving it."

Liat laughs happily and claps again in approval. He doesn't speak much, even though he can. His sisters are the opposite, they never shut up.

"Auntie Rose says she's going to teach them how to make pancakes," Lily says with a chuckle. "I told her they're a little young for that, but she says they need to learn how to feed themselves if their parents are away on jobs. She seems to be convinced that your happy-family-at-home-time will end soon."

"No idea why she'd think that," I mutter. "I'm being the perfect housewife."

Lily sniggers. "Of course, you are. Don't think I don't know about the little excursion you did last week. Pumpkin spotted you in town. I just wish you'd have dropped by for a visit."

"I didn't want a lecture. You know the guys insisted on having this one year without any killing." I sigh. "It's getting harder and harder. I miss it, Lily. It's part of me. I'm not made to simply sit at home and play with the litter.

They're getting more and more independent and soon, they're going to want to do their first kills."

"Kat, they're a year old today. They're not going to kill anything for a while. Maybe a mouse at most, and even that I can't imagine. It's not like they're very good at shifting."

Ah, yes. Of course, she has to rub it in. While all four have had their first complete shift, they seem completely helpless as kittens. Like new-borns, basically. Definitely not ready to hunt and kill mice. It's strange how different their development is shifted versus human, but even after a year of trying to find information on cat shifter babies, we've drawn a blank. It's all going to be wait and see. I suppose I've always liked surprises.

"Aunt Rose also said she wants us to come for a visit. Now that Gryphon's sister has moved out, she's got more space in her house. I bet the twins would love to have you over."

"I doubt she'll have enough space for four adults and four children," I say with a smile. "But I'll thank her for the offer nonetheless."

"You really have changed," Lily muses. "When I first met you, you'd never have thanked anyone for anything. Now look at you."

I shrug, feeling a little uncomfortable at that statement. Am I losing my assassin cred? Just because I haven't killed anyone in a while doesn't mean I've turned ordinary. And even if I have learned some manners, so what. I'm still the same old me.

"Mum, Shade's bit me!" Bella comes running and jumps on my lap, ignoring that her brother is already clinging to me. Kids. They have no sense of other people around them.

Liat growls at his sister and wraps his tail even tighter

around my throat. I know he doesn't mean it, but he's getting into strangling territory now.

"What did you do to Shade before she bit you?" I ask Bella, fixing her with a stern glance. I don't believe for a second that little Bella is innocent. She may look like a fanged angel, but she's a little demon inside, just like all four of them.

"She took the last piece of chocolate cake!" Shade shouts, running towards us. "Mum, I wanted chocolate cake!"

"So did I. Who's eaten it all?"

Bella points at my guys. Gryphon's lips are dark with cocoa powder. Traitors.

"We're going to force Caitlin to make us another cake, alright? Just for us girls."

Liat growls again. "Yes, and for you. And if Lily comes to visit, she gets a slice too."

"I appreciate it," Lily chuckles. "Don't worry, I'm planning to visit again soon. It's getting less busy now that we've got M.E.O.W. up and running again. Benjamin's been great with getting on top of the bills, by the way. Maybe give him a raise. Feeding that deer of his must be expensive."

"A raise? What do you think I am, a nice boss?"

"The best. Now hand me my little nephew and get yourself some cake before it's all gone. A party isn't a party without a belly full of cake."

I hand her Liat and head over to the buffet, followed by my girls. I scan the garden for Donna until I find her sitting with Sophie and the twins. Looks like she's trying to be part of the cool crowd. This is the first time Sophie's met Ivy and Four, and they've immediately become the best of friends. I told them yesterday not to comment on her missing eye, but it wouldn't have been necessary. Living with Aunt Rose has been good for the twins. They seem younger, more carefree now. Hopefully, they'll be able to regain their lost childhood, just like Sophie. Caitlin sits nearby, watching her younger siblings. Pumpkin is by her side, talking rapidly. I could concentrate and listen to what he's saying, but I'll leave them their privacy. The two teenagers have been growing close – it's adorable. Young love at its best.

"Kat, we saved you some truffles!" Lennox waves a cellophane bag. Yummy. I'm by his side in an instant.

"Do they contain catnip?"

"No, but I may have some catnip biscuits hidden in my pocket." He grins. "They cost one kiss each."

"That's extortion!"

"No, it's business. Would you like one?"

He snakes an arm around my waist and pulls me close.

"How can I resist - even with those abhorrent prices."

He laughs and pulls out a biscuit. It's already crumbled away at the edges. It's high time it lands in this cat's greedy stomach. I open up wide and he feeds me, chuckling when I lick his fingers. I munch the biscuit with delight, purring a little when the catnip rush hits me.

I want to *rub* something. The urge to rub against a leg is so strong that I drop to the ground and press myself against Lennox's leg. I push against him, rolling from side to side, completely oblivious to the world. This is the best state of cat.

HOURS LATER, WHEN THE CHILDREN HAVE GONE TO BED, it's just the guys and me. We sit on a large fallen tree in the garden, enjoying the pleasant night air. It was there when we bought the house and we never bothered to have it removed. It makes the perfect bench, big enough for all four of us. The sounds of the forest are soothing, reminding me once again that we're in our own little paradise.

Ryker snakes his arm around my waist and I lean my head on his shoulder, exhausted from the long day of partying. Gryphon yawns, clearly having the same sentiment.

"The stars are beautiful tonight," Lennox says quietly, craning his neck back. "It's the new moon. That's when they're always the brightest."

Ryker points at a group of stars to our right. "Back when I thought I was a cat, we called that constellation the Great Purr. If you draw some lines between the stars, it looks like the sound a purr makes."

"How does a sound look like a purr?" Gryphon asks, echoing my confusion. "Don't tell me cats have an alphabet?"

"We see the world a little differently from others. Sometimes, sounds form images." He shrugs as if that's supposed to make sense.

I stare up at the sky, trying to see a purr. It's ridiculous, but it's not the weirdest thing we've ever done.

"I think there's a meow over there," I say after a while and point to a particularly bright star. "Yes, definitely a meow."

Ryker elbows me in the ribs. "I was serious."

"So am I." I laugh. "Or maybe not."

We sit there in silence, enjoying each other's company under the sparkling night sky, until Lennox shouts out in excitement.

"Look, a shooting star!"

He's right. Not just one. An entire swarm of shooting stars paint streaks across the darkness.

"Make a wish," my wolf whispers.

I think for a moment, then I turn and smile at him.

"I don't need to. Life is exactly how I want it."

THE END

If you enjoyed this story, please take a moment to leave a review.

If you want some catnip, subscribe to my newsletter: skyemackinnon.com/newsletter

And if you want to know more about how the sirens came to be, read on for a sample of Song of Souls, set many years before the events in Catnip Assassins.

Finally, I have written a bonus scene about the moment Pumpkin first shifted. You can find it here: skyemackinnon.com/pumpkin

Dear readers,

I hope you enjoyed this final book in the Catnip Assassins series. It was a hard one to write – maybe the hardest book I've ever written. Kat didn't want it to end. She fought me at every turn. She stopped talking, she sulked, she threw a hissy fit. It took longer than planned to wrangle her into submission and make her tell me the last bits of her story.

What helped a lot was my cat Sootie. She's all black, sneaky, manipulative and has sharp claws – remind you of someone? She's inspired a lot of the cat scenes in this book. She also deleted an entire scene by lying down on my keyboard for a nap – thank goodness for cloud backup.

Even though it's only been one and a half years since Meow was published, it feels a bit like the end of an era. Yes, I'm being overly dramatic, but still... So many new readers have found their way to my books because of the Catnip books. You have shared your cat pictures, drawn cats, suggested names, reviewed the books, recommended them, even written blog posts about them. You, dear readers, are why there are now seven books instead of the one I'd originally planned.

So, thank you. If you've read Roar, you're one of Kat's superfans and I hereby give you a socially distanced hug.

I'd also like to thank my wonderful betas and ARC readers. And my Flock friends who endured me posting snippets in our Whatsapp chat way too often. And my PAs, past and present, who've been part of the Catnip journey. And my family, who've started to read the series too (no, mum, Kat didn't decide on one guy and she never will, no matter how much you beg me to!).

As mentioned at the end of the epilogue, there is a bonus scene about Pumpkin. I'm also planning to one day write a book about his adventures, but not right away. There may however be a Catnip holiday story coming in time for Christmas – keep an eye out. Of course there's no Christmas in Kat's world, but they do have a different winter celebration… spoilers.

For now, let me wish you all the best during these strange times. Thank you for reading Kat's story.

Meow!

Skye MacKinnon

October 2020

(in case you read this many years from now when the Covid-19 pandemic is just a distant memory)

Nobody can resist his call.... not even her...

The Piper's music is alive, drawing souls from the world of the living to the domain of Death. Those who hear him have no choice but to follow - when the Piper calls you, you will do as you are told.

Everything changes...even the unchangeable...

Autumn is on the run from the Cult of the Hundred after witnessing something she should never have seen. She's fighting for survival; she doesn't have time for distractions.

That is, until she meets a man nobody but her can see. When he speaks, her body does what the Piper commands, but she's not going to accept that. Not at all.

A new song has begun...

He's played his tune for a hundred years, but no living human has ever seen him. Until Autumn. His music is only supposed to control those destined to leave this world, but to make Autumn stay with him, he might have to change the rules. Forever.

PROLOGUE

It has been one hundred years since our children left.
Mothers wept.
Families were torn apart.
They all searched for them.
Not a single child was ever found.
And amongst it all, the question, the oldest question
there is.
Why?

HIM

Time has lost all importance. It's a leaf on the wind, carried away into oblivion.

Only the music counts. The Song guides me from town to town, compels me to do my work before leading me to the next place. It has been one hundred years since the day I first set foot on Earth, yet most of the time it feels like only a day has passed. Only sometimes do I feel the heavy burden of time, when I give in to the very human sensation of boredom.

Every day follows the same pattern. It is reassuring that way. I don't have to change my ways. The Song never ends. And on and on I go, travelling the land, never seen, never noticed. Even the humans with the Song inside of them can't see me. They follow my call, eager and willing, yet they never get to know who's herding them to their destiny.

I'm not a vain person, yet sometimes, I wish they could see me. I have not spoken to anyone since I was placed in this world. *Lie.* I have spoken to humans, whispered into their ears, but they never reply. They cannot hear me. I exist in the corner of their eye, in the shadows they fear, never seen. Some feel my presence, a shiver running down their back, the feeling of being watched, but none of them *sees* me.

I understand why it has to be that way. They would never follow my call if they knew it was me. Most of their stories are wrong, but they have described my looks in many of them. The horns, the glowing eyes that resemble burning coals. I am not the devil in their fairy tales, but I certainly look like him. For a while, I styled my beard into a goatee to match their descriptions, but that got boring after some time since nobody could see it anyway.

Today, the Song leads me to a village I've not been to before. That is becoming increasingly rare. It's a small hamlet, no more than twenty houses, all of them huddled together in defence of the wild lands surrounding it. It's taken me an entire day on horseback to reach it. A hundred years ago, I travelled on the back of the music, faster than the wind, but I have become tired of that recently. I wished for a horse and it came into existence, a large, black steed with fiery eyes and an insatiable appetite for apples. He doesn't need earthly food, just like myself, but apples help motivate him on dreary days like today. I have a couple of them stashed in the saddlebags, in case he throws yet another tantrum. He's a magnificent stallion, but he's also strong-willed and temperamental. Some days, I leave him in the stable and later wish him to wherever I've ended up. He doesn't like it, but it's not like I care.

I stopped caring a long time ago.

The village's gloomy atmosphere makes me want to move on and find a prettier place, but the Song doesn't allow for that. If I don't follow it, it'll make me pay. The Song is always hungry, always looking for its next victim, and I'm its tool, nothing more. The Song decides who I will lead from this world and into the next. I can't resist it any more than the humans can.

I jump off my steed and offer him another apple. There's no need to bind him to a tree; he won't leave. He knows I'd just wish him back to wherever I am. He's more intelligent than mortal horses, although I sometimes wish that wasn't the case. He judges me for what I do, I know it. His fiery eyes hold disappointment whenever the Song leads me to a child. I've told him that I cannot fight the Song, but his disdain for my actions doesn't waver.

Just a horse. His opinion doesn't matter.

I walk into the village until I get to the house the Song points out. It's the biggest one with a sturdy, freshly patched roof. I walk through the closed door and two walls until I see the human I'm here to take. An old woman, at the edge of death. Those are my favourites. They don't have long to live anyway. Me pulling them into another world won't change much. It's a very different case when it comes to children. Those are hard.

I take out my pipe and gently stroke it. I love it as much as I loathe it. The music it produces is beautiful, yet I hate what it does to people.

As soon as I hold the pipe to my lips, the song fades. It always does that, now that it's sure I will follow its command. It's like it isn't needed once I play the pipe and create my own music. My fingers dance on the smooth wood without my intervention. I never learned to play the pipe. It's almost like it plays me.

Today's melody is slow and wistful. It matches the movements of the old lady as she gets up from her armchair and walks towards me. Her eyes are blank, enchanted by the music. I don't know if humans are aware of what's happening when they're controlled by me and my pipe. If they are, they don't show any signs of struggle. Most have passive expressions, but some relax, even smile. It makes me feel better about it all.

This woman doesn't smile, but she looks relaxed as if she's dreaming about something nice. No nightmares for her.

I never stop playing as I leave the house, trusting on the old lady to follow me. She shuffles along, barefoot and in nothing but her nightgown. It doesn't matter; her neighbours won't stop her. Once I play the pipe, humans will ignore my victim. They still see her, but they don't care that she's not dressed properly and is randomly walking down the street. It's a strange magic which means that families will never get to say goodbye to their loved ones.

I have to walk slow to match the woman's pace. I want to be away from the village before I turn her over to the Song. It feels wrong to do it in such close vicinity to other humans, even if they can't see me. If they knew I existed, they'd be scared. Their entire lives would be different. They'd know that they could be taken from their life at any moment and that there's nothing they can do about it. Being powerless is one of the worst feelings in the world. I know it all too well.

When we're far enough from the village, I stop and turn around, but don't end my tune. It's turned mournful, tearing at my heartstrings. I may not be human, but I do have a heart. The remains of one, broken and frozen in mid-beat.

I look down at the woman with regret. I can't help what's about to happen. The Song is in control. I'm just the instrument, just like the pipe I'm playing.

As soon as I decide that it's time, the tune changes into something that I can only describe as pure power. It's no more just one instrument playing a melody; it's an entire orchestra and choir that's thundering from all around us, so loud it almost hurts. The air in front of us begins to shimmer until a glass gate appears between the old woman and me. It looks like just an arch, which it is for me, but for her, it's a gate that will take her away from this world and into another.

She still looks like she's sleepwalking. I sigh without stopping my tune. It's time to do what has to be done. The Song is ready.

I stop playing and lower the pipe. The woman's eyes clear and she realises for the first time that she's no longer in her living room. Shock and fear spread across her wrinkled face. I hate this moment. She opens her mouth to scream, but the Song is faster. It grabs her and pulls her through the portal before her scream ever reaches my ears.

As soon as she's through the gate, it disappears. For a blissful moment, there's only silence. I breathe in deep. If only it could last. This is the only time that I get relief from the Song that constantly plays in my head. I wish I could make time slow down, make this last forever.

But no. The Song jerks back into existence, erasing the silence. It's already picked out its next victim and urges me to travel to them as fast as possible. I don't listen to the command. I'll ride there, slowly, at my own pace. The Song will have to wait.

CHAPTER TWO

AUTUMN

The metal roof above me turns the rain into music. A whole orchestra of drums and cymbals plays in the night, making the gloomy shed a little less hostile. I've been waiting for hours for the storm to pass, but it's not getting any better. The night will be over soon and with it, the cover of darkness I need.

When I set off on my journey, I thought it would be safest to travel during the day. I quickly learned otherwise. Now I take advantage of the empty roads at night, riding my rusty bicycle without having to swerve carts and peasants.

Pegasus is resting by my side. The leather on his saddle is torn in so many places that I doubt it'll stay on for much longer. He was old before I stole him, but it's better than walking. I've become adept at tightening bolts, reattaching the chain and patching up punctures. Still, I know that he won't last forever. He's already carried me for hundreds of miles and I'm nowhere near reaching my destination. I may have to replace him soon, but I don't want to think about that. Pegasus is my only friend, and yes, sometimes I imagine him responding to all the stuff I tell him. I'm probably going crazy, talking to a bike, but there are worse things. Starving, for one. My second biggest problem just now.

The shed I took shelter in is empty, not a single tin of food inside. I was luckier yesterday when I found a box of ancient biscuits and a bottle of slightly fermented apple juice in a cupboard in the abandoned house I slept in. I've got some dried fruit in my bag, but I'm keeping those for emergencies. One night of hunger doesn't class as an emergency.

I hum to myself in rhythm to the rain. How I miss my guitar. I would have been tempted to take it with me had it not perished in the fire. Maybe, one day, once I've found a new home, I'll get one again. I think that day is still far away, but who knows. My luck might change. I feel like I deserve a bit of luck for once, but I doubt Lady Destiny sees it that way. She seems to delight in crushing every hope of happiness and safety.

The rain stops at the same time the sun's first rays appear over the hills in the distance. Great. One night wasted. Now I need to decide whether to bunker down here until the evening or risk travelling during the day. I can't afford to linger here much longer. I don't know if they're still hunting me and I don't want to find out the hard way. Better to keep moving.

The sun beckons me outside. I leave the shed and stretch, letting the sunshine warm my damp clothes. Birds sing all around me, celebrating the end of the rain and the beginning of the day. It's a beautiful morning that lets me forget all my troubles for a moment. I smile and close my eyes. Has sunlight always felt this good? I soak it in, staying like that until a bell in the distance disturbs the peaceful sounds of nature.

As pretty as the bell sounds, I can't help but shudder. No matter where I go, how far I travel, the cult has always got there first.

They call themselves the Church of the Hundred, but I see them for what they are. A cult that brainwashes their disciples into following blindly, doing things they would never have done if they hadn't found the Church. Now, close to the anniversary, they're attracting ever more followers.

When I first learned about them, I thought they may be allies. Friends. I realised the opposite was true when they tried to kill me. Now, I stay away from their temples. Their bells are supposed to call for prayer, but for me, they're a warning.

That's the decision made. I'm going to leave even though it's daylight. Maybe I'll be lucky and find a new shelter around lunchtime; that would give me a couple of hours to sleep before darkness falls and I can continue more safely.

As soon as I'm back on Pegasus, I realise how sore my bum is. Yesterday's road was so full of stones and gravel that I'm surprised I don't have whiplash. Hopefully, the ride is going to be less bumpy today. I'm slowly reaching one of the more affluent areas of the countries, which could mean better roads. I don't know for sure though. Before all this started, I'd never been further away from my village than the larger town twenty miles away. All I knew about the world was what I'd read in books and heard from visiting traders. I almost wish I could turn back time and be back in that innocent state. I was happier then, not knowing what horrors hide behind every corner. What moves in the shadows.

The road is muddy and full of puddles. In no time at all, my trousers are drenched all the way up to my waist and their mossy green has given way to a dirty grey. The fabric sticks to my legs as I pump the pedals as hard as I can. I want to get as far as I can before finding somewhere to sleep.

After two hours of pedalling, I still haven't met a single soul. It's unusual, but not unusual enough to worry me. Yet. Maybe there's a local fair going on that keeps everyone busy. I accidentally stumbled upon one two weeks ago and let myself have a bit of fun. The crowds were thick enough for me to disappear within them, just another reveller amongst the many. I'd spent one of my precious coins on a bag of candied nuts; an impulse buy that I later cursed myself for. There had been jugglers and dancers and fire eaters. I smile at the memory. It had been one of the best days of this journey. I hadn't realised how much I'd missed being around other people, even if it was strangers.

I get to a bridge, an arch so steep that I get off Pegasus in order to push him up rather than try and pedal. At the top, I take a moment to stop and look around. With how bad the road has been, I've barely looked up from the muddy ground, afraid I might hit a rock and crash.

Rolling hills spread far into the distance, painted a myriad shades of green. Any painter would be jealous of this colour palette. The road snakes its way around the hills, staying mostly level; perfect for Pegasus and me. Far away on the horizon, a city rises above the hills. I'm not sure what city that may be, but it's a big one. I think I'm too far south for it to be the capital, but I can't be certain.

I'm going to avoid that city. Yes, I could hide in the crowds, but I'd rather not risk being seen by the wrong pair of eyes. Members of the Church are everywhere. Many wear their black robes to show their allegiance, but not all do. They have spies in all parts of the countries and all levels of society. I learned that the hard way.

The river beneath the bridge is roaring furiously, fed by last night's rain. Foam swims on top of the rapids, reminding me of whipped cream. My mouth waters. I'm hungry already, but I need to ration my food. Later, I promise myself, when I've found a place to bunker down.

I scan the landscape again in search of other settlements. There are no houses or even shelters I can see, but a thin curl of smoke rises in the distance. Maybe a farm, maybe more. It's probably another two-hour ride unless the road starts going uphill. Hopefully not. My thigh muscles have become used to the daily strain, but with the little amount of food I'm getting, I don't want to expend too much energy.

With one last look at the gorgeous green hills, I get back on Pegasus and let him roll down the bridge, enjoying the wind stroking my hair. The air is still fat with moisture, giving off that comforting smell of dust after rain. Petrichor. My favourite word.

The further I get, the better the road is becoming. Fewer rocks are getting in the way and I can let my thoughts drift without having to pay as much attention. Not that there is much to think about. I don't want to linger on my past; it's too painful to remember all that I've lost. And my future...I'm not sure if I'll even have one. I can only run for so long. This can't be the rest of my life. Always on the run, always looking back. No.

Instead, I focus on the present. The smell of the flowers lining the road. The sound of crickets hiding in the tall grass that sometimes strokes my legs when I get too close. Birds are singing far in the distance and a murder of crows passes over me, suspiciously quiet.

A bad omen, right? I look up, kind of wishing I was up

there with them, flying so much faster than Pegasus can carry me -

I fly through the air, twisting, landing, crashing. I hit the ground hard. Pain shoots through my body, but before I can even cry out, darkness claims me.

Continue reading Song of Souls.